S0-CXT-531

YOU HOLD THE LEASH.

Trail a team of dognappers. . . .
Perform with your mutt on TV. . . .
Stow away on a spaceship. . . .
Race your dog against the world's fastest. . . .

What happens in this book is up to the choices
you make page by page. You'll find over thirty
possible endings, from silly to sad to surprising.
And it all begins when your folks say you can
finally have a dog. . . .

Ask for these Making Choices titles
from Chariot Books

DOG FOOD
& Other Delights

Susan M. Zitzman
Illustrated by J. William Powell, Jr.

Chariot Books
DAVID C. COOK PUBLISHING CO.

to Sparky, Misty, and Taxi
my son's favorite "relatives"

Chariot Books is an imprint of the David C. Cook Publishing Co.

David C. Cook Publishing Co., Elgin, Illinois 60120
David C. Cook Publishing Co., Weston, Ontario

DOG FOOD AND OTHER DELIGHTS
© 1987 by Susan M. Zitzman for the text and
J. William Powell, Jr. for the illustrations.
All rights reserved. Except for brief excerpts for
review purposes, no part of this book may be
reproduced or used in any form without written
permission from the publisher.

First printing, 1987
Printed in the United States of America
91 90 89 88 87   5 4 3 2 1

Library of Congress Cataloging-in-Publication Data

Zitzman, Susan M., 1955-
  Dog food and other delights.
  (A Making choices book)
  Summary: As a reward for improving his/her
math grade, the reader is allowed to get a dog
and must make decisions about the kind to get
and how to deal with some unusual and some
dangerous situations including stowing away on a
spaceship and trailing a team of dognappers.
  1. Plot-your-own stories. [1. Plot-your-own
stories. 2. Dogs—Fiction. 3. Pets—Fiction] I. Powell,
J. William, Jr., 1964- ill. II. Title. III. Series.
PZ7.Z69Do 1987   [Fic.]   86-19752
ISBN 1-55513-064-X

Caution! This is not a normal book! If you read it straight through, it won't make sense.

Instead, you must start at page 1 and then turn to the pages where your choices lead you. Your first decision seems harmless enough—will you invest your money in a purebred dog or settle for an easygoing mutt? But soon you may find yourself headed for some unusual and even dangerous situations.

If you want to read this book, you must choose to **Turn to page 1**.

You run in the kitchen door of your home with your report card clutched in your hand. "I did it, Mom!" you yell.

Your parents promised that if you improved your grade in math by the end of the school year, they'd let you get something you've always wanted. Now it's June, you've brought home a B in math ... and your parents are going to let you get a dog!

The family discusses details over dinner.

"You know, of course, that a dog needs a lot of attention and care. You'll be responsible for that," Dad begins.

"You'll have to clean up after him," Mom adds, "and buy his food from your own money." She looks at your father, and they ask the next question in unison.

"Are you really sure you want to do this?"

"YES!!!" you yell, and your little sister, Jenny, chimes right in with you. She's not old enough to take care of a pet, but she's glad you'll have one around.

"All right," Dad says. "We will give you $50.00 toward the purchase and care of your new dog. If you want, you can get a free or cheap puppy somewhere, and use the money for food and shots. Or you can put the money with your own savings and buy a purebred."

Choices: You decide you'd be happy just getting a mutt (turn to page 2).
You'd really like a purebred (turn to page 3).

"I don't want any fancy kind of dog," you finally announce, as the family eats dessert. "I just want a nice dog. One that will be fun and a good friend."

"That's fine," Dad says. "Now we just have to look around for inexpensive dogs."

Jenny pipes up. "My friend Stephanie's dog had puppies a month or so ago. They're cute! Stephanie says they're going to *give* them away to good homes."

"Puppies are a lot of work," Mom says. "If you want, you can get an older dog at the animal shelter for a small fee. They pick up stray dogs and try to find homes for them. If they don't find a place for a dog within a couple of days, they have to kill it."

Choices: You decide to go to the animal shelter and rescue a dog from certain death (turn to page 9).

You want to check out Stephanie's puppies (turn to page 4).

You want to put the money you get from your parents toward the purchase of a purebred dog. The next day you pay a visit to the local pet store to see the various breeds.

The owner, an olive-skinned man with black hair and a foreign accent, is very helpful.

"You must think of many things before you choose a dog," he explains. "Would you like a popular breed? Or might you want a very unusual dog, one perhaps to enter in shows or races?"

Choices: You've always liked being different. You decide you'd like a dog that's out of the ordinary (turn to page 5).
You figure that popular dogs got to be popular because they really make the best pets—and that's what you want (turn to page 10).

The next morning, your sister leads you and your mom over to Stephanie's house. Stephanie takes you to the basement.

Two pups have already been given away, and you look down at two wiggly puppies remaining. They're so small! One is brown like the mother, and the other is completely black. For some reason, you like the little black one right away.

Stephanie's mother comes in then, and your mother asks a question you hadn't thought of. "Who fathered these pups?"

"We don't know," Stephanie's mother admits. "The black pup may be a clue, though. There's a big, black Labrador around the corner...."

Your mother hastily pulls you aside. "Those puppies are cute now," she says, "but if they take after the father, they could grow up to be huge! I just want you to consider that."

Choices: You take the black puppy anyway (turn to page 6).
You decide to look at the animal shelter instead (turn to page 9).

"So, you want an unusual dog," says the pet store owner. "Good. But a pet store is not the place to get such a dog."

"It's not?" You're confused.

"No. You will want to go to a kennel. Each kennel raises only one kind of dog, but they do it very well. I know just the dog you want."

"What kind is that?"

The man's eyes light up. "A truly noble dog, a royal dog. It is tall and straight, and has long fur of great beauty. Not only that, but it is one of the swiftest of all dogs, and a good hunter, too. I will show you a picture."

You peer eagerly as the man reaches beneath his counter and holds out a photograph.

"The Afghan hound," he says proudly. "I myself run a kennel and breed these dogs."

You barely hear what he's saying, you're so surprised by what you see. The dog in the picture is tall and long legged, its body covered with long, golden fur. On top of its powerful neck, eyes and long nose stick out from the midst of another mop of golden fur.

It reminds you of the greyhound dogs you've seen painted on the sides of buses—but wearing a wig. Or maybe it's a sheep dog on a diet.

Choices: You make an appointment to visit the kennel (turn to page 8).

You're not so sure you want an unusual dog after all. You ask the man about something more traditional (turn to page 10).

Your mom sighs. "He is cute," she agrees. "But we can't take him home yet. We have a lot of preparations to make."

You arrange to pick up the puppy that evening; then you speed home and get to work. You have to collect bedding, food, toys. . . . You ride your bike to the local grocery store and pick up puppy food, a dog bowl, and a chew toy, plus an orange crate to use as a bed.

Back home you put the crate in one corner of your room and cushion the bottom with some old towels your mom gives you. You also put in a big, old alarm clock. You've heard that the ticking of a clock is comforting to a lonely puppy missing his mother's heartbeat.

Finally you're ready to pick up your new pet. You take one towel with you and rub it around his old pen, hoping the scent will comfort him later tonight when he wants to sleep. You wrap the puppy in the towel and carry him home.

The puppy acts a little uncertain about his new surroundings until you give him his food. He

wolfs it down happily. You spend the evening playing with him on the kitchen floor—and dashing outside with him occasionally to keep him from making puddles on the linoleum!

All too soon Mom says, "Time for bed." You set the puppy down in his bed and wind up the alarm clock and put it next to him. Then you get ready for bed and crawl under the covers—but not for long.

"Owoo! Ow, ow, owooo!" The puppy is obviously not happy. His cries wring your heart.

Maybe he's cold, you think. You trot into the bathroom and fill up a hot-water bottle. You place it under the puppy's blankets, and pet him for a minute to soothe him. Then you go back to bed.

"Ooooow! Owoooo!"

Choices: You scoop up the puppy and take him into bed with you (turn to page 31).
You put your pillow over your head and ignore him (turn to page 119).

Two days later you are bumping along a dirt road some miles out in the country.

"There it is!" you shout when you see the sign. It reads:

BADAKHSHAN KENNEL
Dog Boarding and Training
Specializing in Afghan Hounds

"Ba-dak . . ." You try to say the name.

"I think your dog seems pretty exotic already," your mom comments, "and I haven't even seen him yet!"

At the door, you meet the pet shop owner again: Daud Sherzad. Mr. Sherzad takes you through several large kennels with indoor pens for feeding and sleeping and fenced-in areas outdoors for play, running, and training.

You see Afghan hounds of all ages, sizes, and colors. The puppies don't look that unusual, but the adult dogs are tall, long nosed, and long-haired, just like the photo you saw. They're bigger than you thought, too. The head of a full-grown Afghan comes up to your chest!

"These are all very fine dogs," Mr. Sherzad is saying. "However, not all of them are show dogs or racing dogs. Do you know yet what you want to do with your dog?"

Choices: You want a dog to enter in dog shows (turn to page 54).

You want a dog that can run in races (turn to page 14).

You just want a dog as a companion (turn to page 25).

The next day, your mother drives you and Jenny to the animal shelter. She points to a blue van parked by the door. "That's one way they get the animals here," she said. "They pick them up off the street. Some are just lost, and others were thrown out of their homes."

Inside the shelter are rows of cages holding cats and dogs. Many look thin and tired. It's a sad sight.

Suddenly, one dog catches your eye, though you can't explain why. He's older, yellowish brown, and rather ugly. One of his ears has a ragged edge, as if torn in a fight long ago. The dog's big brown eyes lock with yours.

"Come here and look at this cute puppy!" your sister squeals from another aisle. But you can't seem to budge.

Turn to page 12.

"So, you would like to see some more traditionally popular dogs," says the pet store owner. "Let's think about size first."

"Hmm. How about sort of middle sized?" you ask.

"Good," he says, leading you to a cage. "Here is one of our most popular dogs—the beagle." With its short hair and long, floppy ears, the pup looks like Snoopy.

"The beagle was originally bred to hunt rabbits," the man explains. "He'll have a good nose."

It's not the nose you're noticing right now. The little brown-and-white, spotted pup has his head tilted to one side and is looking at you with sad brown eyes. It's as if he's saying, "Please take me home!"

That does it. You arrange to pick him up later.

At the pet shop that night, your whole family falls in love with the beagle. Meanwhile you have more decisions to make—toys, teething strips, grooming brushes, collars, travel cages . . . But you're spending so much just for the dog that you pass up even a collar and only get a couple toys.

At home, your pup sniffs his way around his new environment. You soon learn that your new brown and white spotted friend is loving, but not wimpy. He can switch from snuggling and licking to a mock battle if you growl and show you want to play rough. In fact, he likes wrestling so much you name him Hogan, after the wrestler on TV (though your sister hates the idea).

You take Hogan out in the front yard that afternoon, and he happily follows new scents while the neighborhood kids watch. When an orange van marked Animal Shelter drives by, you wave. You could have gotten a dog from them, but you're happy with Hogan.

As the day wears on, the other kids go home, and the air grows cooler. You decide to run in to get a sweatshirt. "Stay here. I'll be right back," you say to Hogan.

But when you dash back out, you don't see the pup anywhere!

You head down the deserted street on your bike, scanning the yards and sidewalks. As you swing around the corner, you see a few kids still outside playing kickball—some of the same ones who just visited your yard awhile ago. You're embarrassed to admit that you've lost your dog already.

Choices: You wave and ride by (turn to page 18).

You ask if they've seen Hogan (turn to page 15).

"You've got to be kidding," Jenny says, when she sees the dog you've chosen, but you're firm in your decision.

"Someone else will take that puppy home, I'm sure," you tell her. "But this dog won't be so popular. He'll end up getting killed, and I don't want him to. I just know he's special."

Your mother gives you a warm smile.

You decide to name your dog Muddy, because of his color. He dozes off on the kitchen rug and whines in his sleep.

"He's having bad dreams," mom says. "It looks to me like he's had a pretty rough life. Maybe his previous owners beat him."

You decide to keep Muddy on the floor in your room that night. The dog continues to whine in his sleep, and every time he does, you lean over and try to comfort him. In the morning, you're pretty tired.

Muddy's second night is much the same as the first. He whines; you pat him; then you both go back to sleep—till he whines again. You're just falling back on your pillow for the umpteenth time when you hear a voice.

"Thank you." You're so tired—you must be imagining things.

Choices: You roll over and go back to sleep (turn to page 27).
You turn on the light to investigate (turn to page 30).

As soon as the words are out of your mouth, you regret them. Trisha wilts like a flower under a scorching sun. Limply she throws the ball back to the pitcher.

You brush your arm across your brow and turn to prepare for the next pitch. As you look at the batter, you notice Midnight, still tied up behind home plate. You remember your mom's comments about praise instead of criticism.

Choices: **You decide to talk to Trisha (turn to page 66).**
You think it's time Trisha realizes she doesn't really belong on a softball team (turn to page 95).

'I'd like a dog to race!" you tell Mr. Sherzad.

He strides over to a pen and lifts a black puppy out. "This little fellow is the one for you," he says. "His father was very swift, so it's in his blood."

You look at the pup's long legs. He looks good to you! You pay Mr. Sherzad for him, and he gives you a pedigree: the pup's ancestry back to his Persian great-great-grandparents.

"Jet black," Dad says with a whistle when he first sees the pup's coat.

"That's it!" you exclaim. "I'll call him Jet."

You train Jet just as you would any puppy, but you also encourage his running whenever you can. Not that Jet needs much urging—he loves to run. He jogs with you every day. You throw things for him to fetch. As he gets older, you go to the high school track and teach Jet to run around the oval and jump the hurdles.

Soon you learn that an Afghan race will be held on the other side of town at a special dog racetrack. It's your big chance to see just how good a runner Jet is. You buy him a red "Racing silk" and a wire muzzle to wear.

The track looks like a miniature horse track, complete with a shorter version of the starting gates. You put the number 3 on Jet's red silk and put him in Gate 3, as instructed.

Choices: You put the muzzle on Jet (turn to page 73).

You decide to leave the muzzle off (turn to page 19).

The ball game stops immediately.

"What happened?" asks a girl named Mindy. As soon as you explain, she comes up with a plan. "We can each search a different yard."

In just a few minutes, she yells, "Here he is!"

To your surprise, there's Hogan—loping up the walk to the front door of your own house, with Mindy behind him.

You dash over and grab him for a big hug. "Where have you been, you rascal?" you ask. "I was worried about you! You could have gotten lost or hit by a car or something."

Mindy sits down on your steps. "At least Hogan has a smart nose," she says.

"A *smart* nose?" you echo.

"Sure! I found him in the bushes next door, but he squirmed away and went right for your house! He was finding his way home by smell. My grandfather has hunting dogs, and he says some dogs have smarter noses than others."

"Well, I don't want to depend on just his nose to get him home," you say. "I'm going to get him a collar right away."

"Good idea." Mindy gets up to go home. "By the way, you can train Hogan's nose if you want—not just to hunt, either. He could take lessons on tracking and searching for things, like missing persons."

A tracking dog sounds exciting. You take Hogan back inside. At least you found out about his nose without losing him in the process!

THE END

"Oh, Mom," you burst out, "Hogan ran away! I lost him! He's outside, but I don't know where!"

You've never seen her move so quickly. She calls Dad from the basement and Jenny from her room and then organizes the neighborhood kids in a yard-to-yard search. You go onto the surrounding blocks, calling and looking, way past suppertime and into the evening. Finally your folks say it's time to quit.

As you eat a late meal, Dad tries to console you. "Someone probably found Hogan and turned him in somewhere. We'll check a few places."

On your way across town to the police station, your car stops at a red light next to an orange animal shelter van. "Why don't you ask them, Dad?" you say.

Your dad talks briefly with the driver and

returns to your car, shaking his head. "The guy said he hasn't seen your beagle—but then, he wasn't in our part of town today, anyway."

"But he was!" you say.

Your dad is saying, "There's the police station," and doesn't respond. At the police desk, they know nothing about your dog. They have you fill out some forms.

"We'll call you if we hear anything," the clerk offers.

"What do you want to do next?" Dad asks you. "We could drive over to the animal shelter and look, or we could go home and phone the shelter from there."

Choices: You want to visit the shelter (turn to page 34).

You decide to go home and call (turn to page 47).

After you've circled the area with your bike and seen nothing, you decide to look for Hogan on foot. You walk through the nearby yards and poke through the bushes.

Nothing.

Hogan could have gone in any direction. If he went through someone's backyard, he could be on another street by now. You're so scared and worried you could cry.

You wander into the kitchen and plop down at the table. Your mom says, "Hi! Where's Hulky—I mean Hogan?"

Choices: You say casually, "He's in the front yard, I think" (turn to page 23).

You know you have to tell her the truth (turn to page 16).

You know the muzzles are to keep the dogs from biting each other, but Jet is no fighter. Besides, he really hates wearing it!

You have just gone into the stands to watch the race when someone yells, "Who brought #3?"

It's the man who organized the race, calling from the starting gates. You rush back down.

"You gotta muzzle your dog, kid," he says. "It's really much safer that way."

"All right," you say with a shrug, "but give me a couple of minutes. Jet hates this thing."

The man looks at his watch. "I'm afraid I'll have to pull you out of the race, then," he says. "We can't wait. Go home and work on getting him used to the muzzle."

Your protests do no good. Sadly, you remove Jet from the racing stall and take him up to the stands with you. It's still exciting to see the long-legged Afghans bounding around the track, leaping the hurdles, and heading for the finish line. Soon one proud owner is collecting a blue ribbon. You wish you knew how Jet would have done.

"Beautiful, weren't they?" says a woman next to you. "Some folks think Afghans are as fast as greyhounds. They can do twenty-five miles per hour! Why—"

Suddenly she gasps and gropes on the bench next to her. "My purse! It's gone!"

Turn to page 122.

You pay Mr. Sherzad for Lapis Lazuli. He hands you her pedigree, papers showing her Afghan ancestry.

At home you begin the hard work of training and grooming Lapis to be a show dog. She can enter a show in the puppy class at six months. Before then you have to house-train her just as you would any puppy. You also have to get her used to walking on a lead, posing in her "show stance," having her teeth examined and her coat brushed, and more.

Fortunately, Lapis is a natural. She's smart and patient and likes people.

The weeks fly by, and in no time you find yourself at the county fairgrounds for your first dog show. Hundreds of people are milling around, and so are hundreds of dogs: large and small, on leashes, in cages, running loose, jumping, barking, yipping, whining.

You lead Lapis through the chaos, clutching the tickets and identification cards you received when you registered. Your father carries Lapis's brushes and towels and a table to groom her on. When you find an empty spot in the grooming area, he sets up the table. Then he goes to find out when and where Afghans will be judged.

You put Lapis up on the table and brush her. She pants in the heat, looking curiously at the bulldog on one side of her and the poodle on the other. You pull out the jug of water you packed and give her a drink. You wish you had a drink, too. You tie Lapis to the grooming table and go to buy one.

You're on your way back with a big cup of Freezy Slush when you notice a crowd around your table. You rush over and find your dad holding a bedraggled Lapis. Near him, an angry-looking young woman has a firm grip on a very excited toy poodle.

When you come closer, you see that Lapis has a scratch on one leg. She won't win any prizes in that condition. She gazes at you dolefully, as if she realizes it, too.

"What happened?" you gasp.

"I wasn't here," Dad says wearily, "but this lady claims Lapis lured her poodle off the table and into a fight."

The woman gives you a nasty look. "My little Genevieve is so upset that I doubt she'll perform in the ring," she says. "It's all your dog's fault."

Choices: You tell the woman she's crazy (turn to page 44).

You apologize to her (turn to page 62).

After that third night, Muddy never whines in his sleep again. But in the daytime, he seems more and more restless. His brown eyes often seek yours, with the same piercing gaze that you first noticed at the animal shelter. It makes you uncomfortable.

One day, you let Muddy out to run around in the backyard. A few minutes later, when you go to check on him, the yard is empty. You see that a hole has been dug by the gate.

"Muddy! Muddy!" You walk around the neighborhood looking for your dog, but it's no use. He's gone.

"Don't feel too bad," Dad says that night when he hears the story. "I think Muddy isn't the kind of dog to stay in one place for long. He's a runaway. That's probably how he ended up in the animal shelter to begin with."

But you're not so sure. You have a strange feeling that Muddy was no ordinary dog. You could see it in his eyes. He had wanted you to do something for him. You just never figured out what it was.

THE END

"He's in the yard, I think," you say casually, trying to look as if nothing's wrong. What would your parents think if they found out you already lost your new dog?

But Mom isn't buying your act. "What do you mean, you *think* he's in the yard? You'd better go out there with him; we don't have a fence."

"Uh, sure, Mom," you mutter and shuffle back outside. You halfheartedly poke through the bushes till dinnertime. At the table, when Jenny asks about the pup, you're forced to tell the truth: Hogan is gone.

Your parents are furious.

"If you'd told the truth, we would have helped you search for him immediately!" Dad exclaims. "As it stands now, I don't think our chances of finding him are very good."

That night you lie awake in bed a long time. The next time you get a dog, you'll keep track of him more closely. But before that next time comes along, you'll have to prove yourself trustworthy to someone else—your parents.

THE END

Your mom is pretty upset the next morning, when she learns the dog slept with you again. Your dad seems disappointed in you.

"But, Dad, I was so tired!" you explain.

"You still need to be firm," he says.

But you don't find disciplining easy. As the puppy gets older, he seems to find more ways to get into trouble. He climbs on the couch, digs holes in the yard, begs for food. . . .

One afternoon, you find your new leather loafers all chewed up. It's just one more item to think about: keeping your shoes shut in the closet, or giving the puppy his own old shoe to chew on, or both. . . . But you're not sure you have the energy to do all that anymore.

That night you tell your parents you'd like to give the dog away.

"I hope you've learned something from all this," your mother says. "It's not easy raising a pet . . . just like it's not easy raising children."

"Maybe I'll be ready for a dog when I'm older," you say. "And, by the way—thanks for not giving *me* away when I was hard to handle!"

THE END

"I'm just looking for a friend," you say.

Mr. Sherzad smiles and leads you to a pen where several puppies are sleeping. One in particular catches your eye, maybe because of its color: a beautiful red gold. You point it out, and the kennel owner scoops up the pup and hands it to you. It snuggles into the crook of your arm and goes back to sleep.

"He's a fine little fellow," Mr. Sherzad says.

You agree. With your free arm you reach for your money, and the sale is made. Mr. Sherzad also gives you the pup's pedigree: his ancestors back to his great-great-grandparents.

You look over the papers. "These dogs sure have strange names."

Mr. Sherzad laughs. "That is because they are *Afghan* hounds, from Afghanistan. I, too, am from Afghanistan."

You wrinkle your forehead. "Afghanistan. I don't even know where it is!"

He smiles again. "My homeland is squeezed between Iran, Russia, and Pakistan. I would love to tell you about it. Perhaps you are interested in our politics? or our religion?"

Your face must register boredom, because Mr. Sherzad comes up with some other topics. "Maybe you would like to hear about spies," he says, "or about guerrilla fighters."

Choices: You want to hear about spies (turn to page 35).

You'd rather learn about guerrilla fighters (turn to page 55).

"See you later, Mom." You head out the door with your mitt in one hand, holding Midnight on his leash with the other, and jog over to the softball field. You enjoy softball, and you're a pretty good player. But not everyone on your team is.

Today your team is practicing with another team that you'll play later, during the regular season. The coaches flip a coin, and the other team gets to bat first. You tie Midnight to the field's backstop and trot out to your position at first base.

You can field a ball well, even when it's coming fast and hard. But then there's Trisha, whom the coach has put in left field. You know for a fact that the kid is afraid of the ball, and she drives you crazy.

Sure enough, the first time a ball comes to her, Trisha shuts her eyes, sticks her glove out— and lets the ball roll right between her feet. You can't believe it.

Choices: "What's the matter with you!" you screech. "That's a ball, not a nuclear bomb!" (turn to page 13).
You bite your lip and keep quiet (turn to page 89).

Muddy doesn't wake up any more that night, and you're able to sleep in peace. The next day he seems to be feeling better, too. He trots restlessly back and forth in the kitchen.

You're still tired from those nights of babying your new pet, so you go to bed early. When you hear Muddy whine, you feel a bit irritated. Fortunately, he quiets down the instant you touch him—as if he just wanted to get your attention.

Then you hear the voice again.

"Thank you."

Am I going nuts? you wonder.

Choices: **You put your pillow over your head and try to go back to sleep (turn to page 22).**

You sit up and turn on your light (turn to page 30).

Your dad carries two large speakers onstage while you waddle out with Midnight and the tape recorder—waddle, because it's hard to walk naturally in a Big Bird costume.

"Go ahead," says a voice from behind a row of bright spotlights.

You clear your throat. "Hi! This is Woofers and I'm Tweeters. We're tweeting for Woofers dog food!" You push "Play" on the recorder, and you and Midnight do your duet.

Afterwards, there's a moment of silence. Then the voice calls, "Next," and you're ushered off the stage. After a few minutes of confusion, someone finally approaches you.

"Well?" you ask expectantly.

"Thank you for your interest in our contest," he says mechanically. "We regret that not everyone can appear in the televised program. . . ."

You're too disappointed to hear the rest of the prepared speech. Dad takes you by the arm and leads you out of the studio. You're halfway out to the car when you notice someone following you, carrying a big bag of Woofers dog food.

"I guess this is the consolation prize," you say as the man puts the bag in the trunk of your car. "Well, my singing and acting career is over. At least it wasn't for nothing."

"Hmmm. Woofers and Tweeters," your dad mutters as he starts the car. "Maybe you have a future in advertising!"

THE END

"I'm sure I heard a voice," you mutter to yourself.

"You did," someone says.

"Who said that?" You look wildly around the room. You can tell no one's hiding in your closet, because the door's open, and nothing's inside but a heap of clothes at the bottom. The voice didn't seem to come from under the bed, either.

Suddenly you realize that Muddy is sitting up and looking right at you with a doggy sort of smile. You peer at him suspiciously.

Then he moves his jaws, and you hear the voice again!

"Yes, it was me," he says. "I was just thanking you for—"

Your eyes are nearly popping out, and you pull the covers protectively up to your chin. "You can't be serious," you gasp.

Now it's the dog's turn to look surprised. "How did you know my real name?" he demands.

"What?" None of this makes any sense at all.

Turn to page 116.

"So, how did the puppy's first night go?" asks Dad at breakfast.

You groan.

"It couldn't have been too bad," your mom comments. "I didn't hear him cry much."

"Yeah, well, he did fine after I took him into bed with me," you explain.

"You did what?" she says. You can almost see visions of dog-scented laundry dancing through her head.

"That really isn't a good idea," Dad says. "I know you felt sorry for him, but you have to be firm. He needs to get used to sleeping alone."

You sigh and nod. "Okay. Can I play with him outside now?"

You keep the puppy out in the yard much of the day. He toddles and wobbles and pounces and rolls and takes a couple of puppy naps. You pick one spot in the yard to be his "potty," and keep carrying him there when necessary, hoping he'll catch on.

When evening comes, you're tired. You hope this night goes better than the last. Gently you lay the pup in the orange crate and crawl into your bed.

"Owowow! Owooo!" He's at it again.

Choices: You put the pillow over your head, determined to make the pup get used to his bed (turn to page 119).
You're too tired to fight it; you take the puppy into bed with you again (turn to page 24).

Sirius motions to you to follow. "Stay low, so you won't be seen," he whispers.

You crawl along the side of the house and into the backyard. There it is; it's brown, with an arched doorway and a shingled roof!

"Looks like a regular old doghouse to me," you say.

"Not on the inside," says Sirius.

Turn to page 86.

You and Lapis follow your father to the ring where the Labs are being shown. The judging has already begun; a group of puppies are trotting around the ring. Lapis squirms excitedly.

The two sexes are judged separately in five different classes, beginning with puppies. These are the female puppies. You watch as each puppy's handler puts her into a show pose with head high, hind legs set back, and tail arched up. The judge goes to each one and looks her over carefully. Then he points his finger to indicate a winner—and it's over. The puppies leave the ring, and the Labs for the next class get ready to go in.

Suddenly you notice a dog handler stooping down and wiping something on his animal's coat. He's using some kind of dye or coloring to make his Lab's coat look more black! You know that it's against the show rules to tamper with a dog's natural appearance.

The handler stands up again and glances around uneasily. Now what do you do?

Choices: You talk to someone in the ring about what you saw (turn to page 41).
You keep quiet (turn to page 50).

It's quite dark when you reach the animal shelter, but the building is still open. A young man at the front desk greets you. "I'm Bill. Can I help you?"

You explain one more time about your runaway pup. "We saw one of your vans tonight, and we already asked them about Hogan," you say, "but we thought we'd stop here, too."

Bill smiles. "Well, one van is all we've got, but animals come here other ways, too. I'll go out back and check."

You don't have much hope left, but what you have vanishes when he returns. "Sorry," he says. "We'll call you if—"

"—if you hear anything," you mutter. As you head out to the car, you feel very tired. The animal shelter van is right next to your car in the parking lot, but you can barely see the letters of its sign in the glow of the streetlight. Wearily, you climb into your seat.

Then, suddenly, you pop out of the car again.

"What's going on?" Dad asks.

You don't respond right away; you're staring at the van. Bill said the animal shelter had only one van, so this must be it. But even in the dim light, you can see something important about it.

The van is blue.

Turn to page 117.

"Yes, Afghanistan is a land full of spies," Mr. Sherzad says. "I told you it borders Russia and Iran; it also touches the border of China! That's two superpowers and one oil-rich land, and they all watch each other. Its location is the reason the Soviet army invaded it in 1979. They conquered the capital city, Kabul. But the freedom fighters, the *mujahiddin,* still carry on a resistance from the hills."

You're amazed. "You mean that ever since 1979 the freedom fighters have been battling the Soviet army, and the Soviets haven't crushed them yet? How do they do it?"

Mr. Sherzad smiles proudly. "They can do it because of their religion. And by the way—there are religious spies in my country, too."

Religious spies? Now you've heard everything.

Turn to page 39.

Curious, you open the book. "Wait a minute!" you say. "I can't read this!"

Jahan bursts out laughing. "Neither can I—it's in Arabic."

You grin back. "I think you inherited your father's love of jokes," you say. "See you next week."

In the next few days, you begin to think Dewana is a good name for your dog. He gets tangled up in a roll of toilet paper, attacks your father's slippers, and gets his face stuck in a peanut butter jar. You keep on house-training him. You also do some reading about Muslims.

Soon you're back at Jahan's. The two of you go out in the big yard with your dog and a gold-colored pup of his. "We're going to teach them to sit," he explains, giving you a handful of treats from his pocket. "Just do what I do."

Jahan's pup is standing in front of him. "Sit!" Jahan commands. Then he forces the pup's back end onto the grass. "Good dog!" he says to the bewildered animal, and offers a treat.

As Jahan repeats this process, he motions for you to try it.

"Sit!" you say firmly. You practically have to pull your pup's legs out from under him to get his back end down, but finally he's sitting. "Good dog!" you say, and give him his reward.

After a few rounds of this, you're hoping your pup will catch on. Instead, he's so frantic to get to the treats that he jumps up and knocks you down!

Choices: "You dumb dog!" you yell (turn to page 120).

You ask Jahan for help (turn to page 146).

Your mom comes into the kitchen and looks at you curiously while you spank the dog. Then her expression changes to one of anger. "You stupid kid!" she yells. "That's a crummy way to treat a dog! What's the matter with you, anyway?"

You're so surprised at her tone of voice that you forget the dog entirely. Your mother has *never* talked to you that way.

In an instant, her face loses its furious expression. "I didn't really mean it, honey," she says. "I just wanted you to see how it feels to be called names. Not too good, right?"

You nod your head.

"Now, I'm not saying that you should never hit your dog or scold him. But it's much more effective to praise a dog—or a person—when he does something right than yell when he goofs.

"Here's another hint for you. Take Midnight out every hour or two and praise him when he wets outside. Watch him closely when he's inside. And when you can't watch him, tie him. He won't wet in an area he has to sit in."

"Thanks a lot, Mom," you say. "Sorry, Midnight." You give him a pat. Suddenly you notice the time on your wristwatch. "I almost forgot! Softball practice!"

Turn to page 26.

"You see, nearly everyone in Afghanistan is Muslim," Mr. Sherzad explains. "The Muslims call the Communists heathen because they do not believe in Allah. They have declared a holy war against the Soviets, and they will never surrender. Thousands have given their lives."

You whistle in awe. "How did you happen to come to America, Mr. Sherzad?" you ask. "Did you escape from the Soviets?"

He smiles. "Actually, I escaped from the Muslim spies," he explains. "I am a Christian. Muslims don't like Christians."

Your mother looks surprised. "It's very unusual to meet a Christian from a Muslim country. How did this happen?"

You're listening for Mr. Sherzad's answer when suddenly you feel something warm and wet on your forearm. Your new puppy just had an accident! You go to wash your arm.

When you return, Mr. Sherzad is saying, "My conversion is a long story. Tomorrow a friend is bringing slides of Afghanistan here. Why don't you join us for an Afghan supper?"

You and your mom agree. "Sounds like fun!"

Mr. Sherzad looks at you with a twinkle in his eye. "Since you like spies and guerrillas, how would you like to solve a riddle or a code before tomorrow night? It will give you a clue to the identity of the man showing the slides."

Choices: You ask for the code (turn to page 42)**.**
You want to solve a riddle (turn to page 56)**.**

The walls are wooden, painted brown. The roof is covered with shingles.

"Come look inside!" Sirius calls. You hesitate. You feel a little foolish about crawling in when there might be nothing there but a smelly old blanket and a bone.

"Hey, punk! Whatcha doin' sneakin' around my backyard in the dark!"

You look up and see someone very large lumbering toward you across the yard.

"Oh, no!" says Sirius. "It's Big Ollie, my former owner. He used to beat me!"

"You never told me that!" you gasp.

"You never asked," says the dog. "Quick—climb in and we can blast out of here!"

He doesn't need to urge you, because Big Ollie is close enough now for you to see his greasy, blond hair and mean, blue eyes in the moonlight. You dive for the doghouse door, but as you do, Big Ollie grabs your heel. You crawl inside on your elbows, but he doesn't let go. Soon you're both inside.

And what you see makes you forget your fear of Big Ollie!

Turn to page 64.

You rush over to the ring, where the steward assisting the judge is letting the dogs and handlers in. She makes sure the numbers on the handlers' armbands correspond with her registration list. After everyone has gone into the ring, you approach her.

"Excuse me," you say, "but I think I saw some cheating going on, and I want to report it."

The woman looks surprised. "No one can talk to the judge right now," she whispers. "What did you see?"

You're just explaining about the dye when you notice a commotion in the ring. The judge has come to the man you saw cheating, and seems to be speaking to him sharply.

Soon the ring empties. The judge stops by the steward and mutters, "That guy was trying to camouflage a light spot. Still had black stuff on his fingers!"

The steward grins at you. "I didn't think we had to worry—this judge is pretty hard to fool. But thanks for your concern. You know, my daughter is about your age. She shows dogs, too. Let me introduce you."

"What kind of dog does she have?" you ask.

"Oh, he's pretty unusual," says the steward. "An Afghan hound ... Hey, where are you going?"

You're already on your way to get Lapis and show her to your new friend. The show wasn't a total loss after all.

THE END

Mr. Sherzad writes something on a piece of paper, folds it, and bids you good-bye.

On the ride home, you open the paper. It has four letters on it: N O O R. You try rearranging them a few times, but that doesn't seem to work. It's not a scrambled word.

At home, after your new puppy has whined himself to sleep, you check to see if the letters Mr. Sherzad gave you represent other letters of the alphabet in the same sequence. "Let's see: if N stands for A, O would stand for B. . . . NOOR would be ABBE, and that's not a word. . . . BCCF? CDDG? DEEH?"

That decoding method isn't working, so you go to bed. The next morning you get your puppy used to his new home. You take him outside and praise him when he wets on the grass.

Your mom agrees to watch the pup in the

afternoon while you work on the code. "Maybe *noor* is a word in another language," she suggests. "A reference librarian might know."

You pedal to the library and explain your problem to a reference librarian.

"Hmmm. I'm trained to find information," she says, "but this is a tough problem. There are lots of languages in the world! Do you have *any* idea what language *noor* might be?"

"The man who wrote it is from Afghanistan," you say.

"That helps." She goes to the phone. "I'll call the Department of Eastern Languages at the university." Soon she's back with an answer. "Light. In Farsi, *noor* means light."

Light? What kind of a clue is that?

Turn to page 67.

"Lapis is very easygoing," you sputter. "She would never start a fight. I think your sweet little Genevieve is the real one to blame!"

"Well!" the lady huffs, picking up her poodle. "I'm going to report you and your dog to the show organizers immediately!" She storms away.

"Don't bother!" you yell after her. "We're not sticking around this lousy show anyway!"

The lady keeps on walking. As you turn back to your table, you notice that the people around you have turned away. Only your dad looks you in the eye.

"That was quite an outburst," he says. You can tell he's disappointed in you. "I suspect her dog started the fight, too, but you didn't pick a very good way to discuss it. Remember what it says in Proverbs? A soft answer turns away wrath."

Your temper has cooled now. You reach over to pat Lapis, who licks your hand. "I'm sorry, Dad," you say. "I guess we might as well go home, right?"

"We don't have to," he says. "I don't suppose we should try to show Lapis, but we could watch some other dogs. As a matter of fact, they're judging Labrador retrievers right now."

Choices: You decide to go home (turn to page 57).

You go watch the Labs (turn to page 33).

You follow the adults into the living room to watch the slides. You've always liked to learn about exotic places, and Afghanistan is certainly exotic. Dr. Gruber's slides show vast, dry, treeless plains and towering, snowcapped mountains; brilliantly colored mosques; turbaned men leading camel caravans; women wearing robes and veils, with only their eyes showing.

"Those robes are called *chadri*," Mr. Sherzad is saying. "Muslims are very modest, and also very strict."

When the lights come on after the slides, you see Mr. Sherzad wiping his eyes. "It is hard for me to see these pictures," he says with a sigh. "I miss my homeland. And I weep for my people. So many without Christ, and now suffering under the Soviets, or crammed into refugee camps. . . ."

"Speaking of refugees," says Dr. Gruber, "there's a Christian relief organization sending help to Afghan refugees in Pakistan. And they're having a bikeathon to raise money." He looks at you. "Maybe you'd like to be in it."

"And speaking of Muslims," says Mr. Sherzad, "I go into the Arab section of the city every week to talk and pass out Christian literature." He turns to you: "You might find it interesting to come along."

Choices: You'd love to join the bikeathon (turn to page 61).

You say you'll go with Mr. Sherzad sometime (turn to page 93).

You swallow hard. "Yeah, he needs to learn a lesson," you agree.

"Just take him upstairs and throw him against the wall a couple times," says Hank. "I'll take this kid outside."

Hank gives you a hand to help you up, and Gus starts hauling Diego up the stairs. You can't stand it any longer.

"No wait!" you cry. "I—I don't want him hurt."

Hank looks at you irritably. "Don't be such a softie. Get out of here, or I'll have Gus give you some of the same!"

You hustle down the stairs and outside to your bike. But you don't want to leave the block until you see what happened to Diego.

In a couple minutes, he comes out of the building. From the way he's walking, you know he's bruised.

"Diego, I'm sorry," you say, but he walks right by as if you don't exist.

You don't know what to do but pedal home, realizing that you just might have lost something even more important than a puppy.

THE END

When you and your dad get home, you call the shelter and tell them Hogan's story. You're not surprised when they say they haven't seen him—but they'll call if they do.

Discouraged, you sit down at the kitchen table to start making posters. Your dad and mom help, and soon you have half a dozen notices describing Hogan and offering a reward for any information about him.

The next afternoon after church, you put posters up at the library and several grocery stores. On Monday you go to the local elementary school. Your mother thinks that one of the summer school students might have seen Hogan, and the principal agrees to let you put a poster up on the bulletin board.

You're just leaving the school when a dark-haired boy runs up to you. "I just read your poster," he says with a heavy accent. "I may be able to help you find your dog."

"Have you seen Hogan?" you ask eagerly.

"Well, no," the boy admits. "But I think I know who might have taken him."

You look at him suspiciously. He's not dressed very well.

Choices: You ask him what he means (turn to page 65).

You decide you don't trust him (turn to page 59).

Hank looks back and forth between you and Diego. "Something's fishy here," he says. "For one thing, there's no easy way to get in here. Both these kids came in of their own free will. There was no robbery."

Gus grabs you by the collar. "You lied, you little punk. Now tell me the truth: what did you want to call the police for, anyway? So they could arrest you for trespassing?"

"Um . . . uh . . ." you stammer.

"Wait a minute—I get it," Hank says suddenly. "I think these two were playing detective, Gus. They probably think we're selling drugs or stealing TVs. Let's show them what we're up to. We've got nothing to be ashamed of."

"We don't? Uh, yeah, we don't, Gus agrees. With Hank as your leader, and Gus as rear guard, you march down the stairs. Hank approaches a door that's labeled LAUNDRY ROOM.

As he turns the doorknob, the room erupts with noise—the sound of a dozen or more dogs barking. "You see?" Hank gestures around the room. "No drugs. No stolen TV sets. We're just starting a kennel business. When we've got more money, we'll move to a better location."

You're barely listening. Your eyes are riveted on one puppy—sleeping in his cage, in spite of all the noise around him. Hogan.

Choices: You say, "That's Hogan!" (turn to page 148).

You don't say anything about your puppy (turn to page 139).

You go back to the ringside and take Lapis back from your father. The handlers and female Labs file into the ring, and everyone falls silent.

"Take them around," says the judge.

The handlers lead their charges on a brisk walk around the ring. All the animals are beautiful, with well-formed, muscular bodies and gleaming coats.

"I wonder how many are really as beautiful as they look," you mutter in Lapis's ear.

Now the judge says, "Stack." Each handler stops his Lab and puts her in a show stance, and the judge examines each carefully.

When he gets to the man you saw cheating, you hold your breath. Suddenly a small argument ensues. The judge is pointing to the man's hand and the animal's coat.

You crane your neck to see better. Suddenly you understand! The man had black marks on his hand from the dye. The Lab's coat must have looked suspicious, but her handler's fingers clinched the verdict.

"Yep, these judges don't miss much," remarks the man beside you. "If a dog gets to be a champion, it's well deserved."

You're relieved that that handler didn't win anything by breaking rules. It makes winning a show that much more special to you. "Lapis, someday you'll be a champion, too," you say to your golden pup. "The honest way."

Lapis gives a short bark, just as if she agrees.

THE END

"Where is your ship?" you ask.

The dog seems to blush through his yellow brown fur. "Well, I don't know exactly where it is. I've been trying to find it, but I keep getting lost—and then the animal shelter gets me!"

"A spaceship shouldn't be hard to find," you assure him.

"But it's camouflaged," he says. "As, um, a *doghouse*."

"Great! We'll never find it," you mutter.

"No, wait!" Sirius says. "I have an address: 327 Franklin Street. I just can't seem to find Franklin Street without help.

The next day you check a map for directions to Franklin Street. After supper, you pedal across town, with Sirius loping along at your side. You've never been to Franklin Street before. When you finally get there, its run-down houses look spooky in the fading light. When you reach number 327, you hear yelling and cursing.

"You didn't tell me this was such a creepy place," you say with a gulp.

"You didn't ask," Sirius replies. "C'mon. My ship's in back."

You follow him, ducking under the windows at the side of the house and then crawling on all fours through the grass. There it is. It looks like a perfectly ordinary doghouse to you.

Choices: You examine the outside of the dog-house (turn to page 40).
You follow Sirius inside his "ship" (turn to page 86).

You head off to church the next morning with a plan in mind—one your Sunday school classmates can help with. You can hardly wait for class to be over, and you don't listen much until the end, when your teacher calls your name.

"Huh? What?" you stammer.

"I was asking if you had a prayer request," she says "I can see you have something on your mind.

You gulp. "Does God hear prayers about lost dogs?"

Mrs. Feeney smiles, and the class includes Hogan in their prayer. Afterwards your friends crowd around, asking what happened. That's when you unveil your plan.

"I want to know where that orange van is all day for the next day or so," you say. "We could have a bike patrol, each of us covering certain

parts of town, and keep track of it."

Just as you expected, the other kids like the idea of solving a mystery. You promise to call them that afternoon and tell each one which part of town to cover.

"What about me?" asks Jon.

You hadn't thought about Jon; he gets around in a wheelchair. But suddenly you realize how he can help. "You can be the central switchboard. We'll call in to you whenever we spot the van," you say. And so it's set.

But Sunday afternoon and evening go by without anyone spotting the van at all.

Choices: **You halt the patrol and try something else (turn to page 76).**

You keep the patrol going another day (turn to page 60).

You envision your bookshelf piled with trophies and blue ribbons. "I'd like to enter my dog in shows," you say.

"All right," says Mr. Sherzad. "I will find just the dog for you. Not all dogs can go into the ring. Judges look for physical perfection according to the breed standard written for each dog. I must find you a puppy that can meet this standard."

He steps into one pen, scoops up a golden-haired pup, and brings it out to you. "This girl is a real princess," he says. "I think she could go far if you trained her well."

You cradle the puppy in your arms, and she licks your hand. "I'll take her," you say. "Hmmm. But what should I name her?"

"I have a suggestion," says Mr. Sherzad. "You could call her Lapis Lazuli, after the deep blue precious stone found in the mountains of Afghanistan. Her full registered name would also include the name of this kennel: Badakhshan Lapis Lazuli."

That's a lot of name for a small dog, you think. "All right," you say, "but I'll call her Lapis for short."

Turn to page 20.

"All right," you say, "tell me about guerrilla fighters in Afghanistan. Is there a dictator there or something?"

Mr. Sherzad's brow darkens. "Since 1979, my country has had so-called presidents, placed in power by the Soviet Union. The Soviets are everywhere. They patrol our streets with tanks and their jets strafe our villages. Yet Afghanistan is not conquered! The *mujahiddin*, the freedom fighters, hide in the hills and continue to resist."

Your eyes widen. "You mean the Afghan freedom fighters have been battling the Soviets since 1979?" you exclaim. "And the Soviets haven't wiped them out? What's their secret?"

Mr. Sherzad smiles proudly. "The secret is their religion. They are religious guerrillas in a holy war."

"Religious guerrillas?" Now you're really surprised.

Turn to page 39.

Mr. Sherzad writes something on a piece of paper and hands it to you. It's a Bible reference: Luke 24:31a.

You spend the next morning getting your puppy used to his new home and yard. You take him outside frequently and praise him when he wets on the grass.

Your mom keeps an eye on the pup in the afternoon while you work on the riddle. You get out your Bible and look up the verse: "Then their eyes were opened and they recognized him."

You run to find your mom in the kitchen. "I don't get it," you say. "This isn't a riddle. It's not even a question!"

She reads the verse while your pup jumps excitedly up and down. "I think this is more like a puzzle," Mom says. "We have to guess who the man we'll meet tonight is, based on the verse. So let's analyze it. Who are the 'he' and the 'they' in the verse?"

You look at the verses ahead of verse 31. "*They* are two disciples," you say, "and *he* is Jesus. That doesn't help any."

"All right," says your mom. "What happened in the verse?"

"The disciples' *eyes* were opened, and they *recognized* Jesus. Eyes opened . . . the mystery man could be a doctor. Or, recognizing Jesus— maybe the guy's a minister."

What's the answer? You'll know soon enough.

Turn to page 67.

You and your father lead Lapis to your parked car. You're upset, and it's not just because you didn't win any prizes. You wish you'd kept your mouth shut. You remember something you heard in church: "No man can tame the tongue." They were the apostle James's words. He compared the tongue to fire and to poison.

You wish you could go back to the lady you yelled at and apologize, but you know you'd never find her in the crowd. You'll just have to ask God for forgiveness. You're glad you can count on that, anyway.

THE END

Sirius looks at you gratefully. "Thanks for thinking about my safety even though you'd like to see the ship. You're a good human. I'll never forget you."

"Good-bye," you call softly as the dog runs around the side of the house to the backyard. Slowly you climb the creaky stairs to the front door and ring the bell. There's a quick flash of light in the sky—Sirius is on his way home.

Then the door in front of you opens—just the couple inches that the safety chain allows. It's enough of a crack for you to see a tired young mother with several children at her side.

"You're not the paperboy. What do you want?" she snaps.

What'll you say? The words are out before you know it. "I was wondering—uh, well . . ." you stammer. "Um, our church has a Bible club for children every Tuesday, and—"

"Oh!" the woman exclaims. She unlocks the chain, and the door swings open. "Come on in."

Maybe ringing the doorbell wasn't a bad idea after all.

THE END

What if he's just making up a story to get the reward money?

"I'll check with you in a couple of days," you say, though you don't really plan on it.

"I'll be here," he replies. "My name is Diego."

Over the next few days, your family makes sure that someone is home to answer the phone at all times, but you never get any calls about Hogan. He's just disappeared.

Your dad tries to comfort you. "I think Hogan's alive, at least," he says. "If he'd been hit by a car, someone would have reported it. He's probably been stolen. We'll just have to pray that he's happy and well cared for."

You sigh. "I guess you're right."

You know one thing for sure. If you ever get another dog, you'll put a collar and tags on him.

And you won't let him out of your sight.

THE END

On Monday you pack a lunch so you can be out all day, covering your area. You also get permission to take along the cordless phone.

Just before noon, the phone rings. It's Jon. "The van is heading your way on Hill Avenue," he says excitedly. "Cathy spotted it in the Forest Trails neighborhood, heading north. Then Brett called and said it was going up Hill. He got the license number, too."

"Great!" You hang up and pedal over to Hill Avenue. When you see the van, you note the time and call Jon. By day's end, Jon has a log of the van's movements.

You call the animal shelter and explain your suspicions to Bill. "We spotted it in Forest Trails and Oak Bluff today. Have any dogs been reported missing from those neighborhoods?"

"Why, yes, there have been," says Bill in surprise. He agrees to call the police for you. "No other animal shelter is operating here," he says, "so *something* fishy is going on. Your evidence may be enough to justify a search warrant."

Now all you can do is wait. Several hours go by, and when the phone finally rings, you jump.

Dad answers it and turns to you. "It's the police department. They want you to come down there right away."

"Maybe they're going to put you in jail for harassing innocent people in orange vans," Jenny quips.

Turn to page 72.

You spend extra time biking to get in shape. Sometimes you bike around the high school track and let your puppy run alongside you, even though he's too little to keep up.

You also collect pledges from friends and family—a certain amount of money to be given to the relief work for every mile you pedal.

You're in the garage one rainy day, sanding the rust off your bike's fender, when you decide on a name for your red pup. "I'm going to call *you* Rusty."

When the bikeathon day comes, you tell Rusty he has to stay home. With the other bikers, you travel a prescribed route through town. Your training pays off and you go the full ten miles, as you'd planned. Afterwards, you feel fine. And you know your efforts will help the refugees in Pakistan.

But in the morning, when Rusty jumps on your bed to wake you, you realize your muscles are pretty sore!

"Oh, well," you groan, "I guess this is what people mean when they say 'It hurts good.' "

THE END

You can't imagine Lapis starting a fight with another dog—but you know you carry some of the blame for the scuffle. "I'm sorry this happened," you say. "I don't know who started the fight, but I shouldn't have left Lapis alone. This is her first show." You motion toward the scratch and add, "I guess we'll just go home now, though. What about your dog? Is she okay?"

The woman calms down, though her face is still red. "She seems to be fine. She just gets jumpy with all these other dogs around. I guess she was to blame, too," she admits. Then she extends her hand to you. "By the way, I'm Angela Carson. Don't go home—there's a lot to see here. Why don't you watch me show Genevieve?"

"All right," you agree. "That would be fun." You and Dad and Lapis follow Ms. Carson

through the crowd. When you leave the shade of the grooming area, the sun beats down on you mercilessly. Carrying Lapis makes you feel even hotter.

At the ring, Ms. Carson goes to the end of a long line of people and toy poodles. You notice that her face is still red; you wonder if it's the heat.

You've just turned to look for a place to watch the show when you hear gasps behind you. You whirl around and see someone on the ground. It's Ms. Carson—she's fainted! And in the gathering crowd, little Genevieve looks about to panic.

Choices: **You run to Ms. Carson's side** **(turn to page 78).**
You try to grab Genevieve before she runs away **(turn to page 131).**

You can't explain it, but the inside of the "doghouse" is larger than the outside. You can stand up straight, and so can Big Ollie—but he doesn't stand for long. With a thud, he falls to the floor in a dead faint.

When Sirius hears the thud, he turns with a start. "Oh, dear," he sputters. "I already blasted off trying to escape him! It's too late to go back!"

You brace yourself in the doorway and survey what seems to be the control chamber of Sirius's spaceship. The room is large, circular, and metallic green. Sirius stands at a table in the center—on his hind legs, as if that were his normal posture.

"Too late?" you gulp. "Glad I like to travel."

"Me too," Sirius says. "Let's get you two humans comfortable." He presses a button, and several doorways appear from nowhere.

When you gasp, he explains: "That's just an optical trick. The same kind that disguises a large, round ship as a small, square doghouse. Now, can you help me with Big Ollie?"

The two of you drag the big man through one of the doorways into the sleeping quarters.

"Would you like something to eat?" Sirius asks, motioning to another doorway. "It's going to be a long trip."

Choices: You accept his offer of food (turn to page 100).

Eat dog food? No way! (turn to page 71).

"You think you know who might have taken Hogan?" You echo the boy's words. "I don't understand."

"I live over near the plastics factory," the boy, whose name is Diego, explains. "There's an old abandoned apartment building near us, and sometimes in the evening I hear barking there. A lot of barking. I know there are lots of dogs in that building—maybe someone is stealing them and hiding them there."

You look at Diego critically. It's not much of a clue.

Choices: You decide not to follow up on his lead (turn to page 59).
You pursue his story further (turn to page 96).

Feeling bad about your outburst, you quickly ask God's forgiveness. Then when your team leaves the field to bat, you wait for Trisha and walk in with her.

"I'm sorry I blew up at you," you say. "You were pretty close to catching it that time—you didn't run away or anything. If you keep your eyes open next time, you just might get it!"

She brightens up a bit. "Do you really think so?"

"Just keep on trying," you say. "You'll get there."

Sure enough, the next time a ball goes to Trisha, she keeps her eyes open, and her mitt actually stops the ball. It takes her forever to pick it up and throw it to the second baseman, but you overlook that.

"Way to go, Trisha!" you call out. "You're coming along!"

Your team loses the practice game, but you don't mind too much. You have a feeling Trisha won't be as much of a liability when you play this team in the regular season.

After the game, the coach approaches you. *Oh, no,* you think. *He'll probably scold me for mouthing off.*

Turn to page 85.

At dinner time, you and your parents drive out to Mr. Sherzad's home again. Your sister gets left with a baby-sitter, because the visit might get too late for her, but the little red puppy is with you.

To your surprise, the person who opens the door there is your family eye doctor, Dr. Paul Gruber!

"Well, I can hardly believe my *eyes*! Ha, Ha—a little professional joke," says Dr. Gruber. "Come on in! I didn't know who my audience would be tonight; my friend Daud here likes mysteries." Mr. Sherzad steps out from behind Dr. Gruber.

You pounce on him with your question. "Eye doctor? Is that what I was supposed to figure out from the paper?"

"That's part of it," Mr. Sherzad says with a smile. "But come—let's eat now and talk later."

He beckons you into a dining room, where you see the evening's dinner—and smell its unusual aromas. In the center of the table is a platter of rice, covered with gravy that seems to have chicken and carrots and nuts and something else in it. Raisins! To one side is a large tureen filled with a thick, yellowish soup.

Mr. Sherzad's wife notices your puzzled gaze. "That's pumpkin soup," she explains cheerfully.

Choices: You're willing to try some new foods (turn to page 68).
You say your stomach feels queasy (turn to page 84).

You all sit at the Sherzads' table: Mr. Sherzad, his wife, their two children, Dr. Gruber and his wife, and your family. Mr. Sherzad asks God's blessing, and then everyone digs in.

"Ginger gravy? Delicious!" your mom is saying to Mrs. Sherzad. Whatever it's called, the rice dish is different—but you like it. You try the pumpkin soup, and it's good, too.

During the meal, Mr. Sherzad winks at you and says, "I told you there was more to the mystery than you discovered. The rest of it is this: Dr. Gruber is a spy!"

Everyone at the table gasps—including Dr. Gruber.

"Dr. Gruber was a spy for God," Mr. Sherzad explains. "In the last century, there have only been fifteen years when Afghanistan would allow missionaries in its borders. But many Christians came in other ways: as engineers, teachers, doctors. For a time there was a Chris-

tian eye clinic, NOOR: the National Organization for Ophthalmic Research. Dr. Gruber worked there."

You learn that Mr. Sherzad heard about Jesus from a university professor. It was dangerous for him to become a Christian; many Muslims believe that anyone who turns traitor to Islam should be killed. When the Soviets came to Afghanistan, he knew it was time to leave. He and his family escaped on foot to Pakistan, and then came to America.

"Let's see the slides now," Mr. Sherzad says, "even though they will make me homesick." Everyone heads for another room—except for Jahad, Mr. Sherzad's son, who motions you to follow him.

Choices: You go watch the slides (turn to page 45).

You go with Jahad (turn to page 90).

You ask Sirius many questions about his home planet and his mission to Earth. Sirius explains that his is a follow-up expedition to one that had crashed here centuries ago. Though the dogs of Sirius's race communicated as equals with man for a while, in time they were absorbed into the rest of Earth's dog population. Only some names in Greek and Roman mythology and pictures in Egyptian tombs gave clues that they had come at all.

Sirius finishes the story and sighs. "I'm glad to know that not all dogs here are mistreated, anyway," he says. "My last owners beat me. But I have to get back to their house—my spaceship is there! I need you to help me find it, but I must warn you that it could be dangerous."

Sirius tells you the address of his former owner's house. As the sun sets, you begin your trip. It's dark when you reach Franklin Street. The houses look old and unkempt, and number 327 is the worst of all.

"This is it!" says Sirius. "My ship's in back."

You hear yelling from inside the house. You hate to think what these people might do if they found their old dog, or caught someone snooping around their yard.

Choices: You say you'll ring the doorbell and distract the people so Sirius can have a safe getaway (turn to page 58).
You want to risk seeing the spaceship (turn to page 32).

"Uh, no dinner for me, thanks," you say. You never were very good at trying new foods at restaurants.

"Go explore, then," says Sirius. "You might enjoy looking at the star map in the chart room, two doors down."

You go look at the map, but when you study it, you start to feel a bit woozy. You're not sure if the black screen and white dots are on the wall or in your head. You sway unsteadily just as Sirius enters. He looks at you suspiciously.

"Space travel can be exhausting," he says. "You really should eat dinner. I guarantee you'll find it delicious."

Choices: You say, "All right, what's for chow?"
(turn to page 100).
You say, "Don't worry—I feel just fine"
(turn to page 79).

Your sister was just teasing about jail, but you're still nervous. Cautiously, you open the police station door. . . .

"There you are!" "Sure, that's the kid!" Stampeding toward you are a couple of police officers and Bill, and someone who seems to be a reporter. Bill is carrying something.

"Hogan!" you yell. Soon the puppy is nestled in your arms. A flash goes off; the reporter just took your picture.

"The police used the van's license number to find the owners' address. When they searched the building they found a couple dozen dogs," Bill explains.

"Good work, kid," says an officer. "You saved some of those dogs from death. Purebreds like yours would probably have been sold again, but the mutts—well, there's a black market for animals to use in laboratory experiments. . . ."

"I'd like to hear more about how you solved this mystery," says the reporter.

The next Sunday morning, Mrs. Feeney holds up the newspaper photo and clipping, headlined LOCAL KIDS BUST DOGNAPPING RING.

"See? God did answer our prayers," she says to you. "He gave you an idea, plus people to help you carry it out."

"You're right." You look around at your classmates, and silently say, "Thanks, God."

THE END

Jet hates to be muzzled, and it takes a while to get the contraption strapped over his nose and mouth and fastened around the back of his head. But you know it's a good safety precaution, so the dogs don't snap at each other during the race.

Finally Jet is ready, and you head up into the stands to watch the race. There's a short delay while the race's organizer looks over the stalls to check that the dogs are muzzled.

As you wait, you overhear someone making bets on the race.

"I'm putting five dollars on Big Red," says one man.

"Are you kidding?" a woman's voice retorts. "Ten dollars says my Silver Streak wins by two lengths!"

You feel a sudden urge to bet on Jet. After all, Mr. Sherzad said racing was in the dog's blood.

Choices: You put five dollars on Jet to win (turn to page 113).

You decide not to bet (turn to page 138).

"Sure, kid," the guitar player says. "Just don't drop it!" He hands the instrument to you. It's a real beauty, too. You grip it nervously. After this extra commotion, the audience is watching you more closely.

Just relax, you tell yourself. You begin strumming. The guitar has a beautiful sound, and the audience gives a sigh of appreciation. When you start singing, your voice sounds strong and confident, and Midnight howls along beautifully. "Me and you and a dog named Boo, travelin' and a-livin' off the land . . ."

When it's over, you pass the guitar back. "Thanks very much," you say. Then you walk offstage and listen to the other dogs sing. A poodle yips along with "How Much Is That Doggie in the Window?" A bassett hound croons as his master sings, "You Ain't Nothin' but a Hound Dog."

When all have finished, the host calls everyone back onstage so the audience can choose a winner by applause. He points to the entrants one by one. When he gestures in your direction, the room erupts with clapping and cheering.

"I think we have a winner, folks!" he says, slapping you on the back. "We like your courage, kid!" He hands you an envelope with a check in it, while his assistant passes out T-shirts to the other dog owners.

Then the show is over. The cameras shut down; the audience files out. You hand Midnight's leash to your dad and walk over to where the band members are packing up their instruments.

"Thanks a lot," you say to the guitar player. "That sure is a beautiful guitar; I don't think I would have won without it. Could you give me your name and address? I'd like to send you part of this prize after I cash the check."

"I'm Phil Sanders," says the guitarist. "There's no need to send me a check. It was my pleasure. But you could do something else for me."

"What's that, Mr. Sanders?" you ask.

He hands you his business card. "Think about taking lessons from me. You've got talent."

"Thanks!" you stammer. "I will think about it, I promise." You rush to go find your dad. The TV show is over, but you have a feeling that something else is just beginning.

THE END

You decide to set a trap for the dognappers, to catch them in the act. You choose a partner, someone who has a dog and lives in another part of town.

"Me?" Jon asks from his wheelchair. Soon he says yes, and the two of you plot details.

The next morning you tie Jon's dachshund, Fritz, to a tree in front of his house. Then you lie down behind some nearby bushes, Polaroid in hand and pencil and paper in your pocket.

Jon serves as lookout. He sits up on a small balcony outside his bedroom, armed with a video camera (his idea).

You've been sitting by the bushes about an hour when Jon shouts. "Here comes the van!" You scramble beneath your cover and wait, but the van passes slowly by. You're just sitting up again when Jon calls, "They're coming back!"

This time the van stops. A short, dark-haired man hops out from the passenger side, swiftly cuts Fritz's leash, and picks the dog up. You press the button on the camera.

Errzeep! You never realized a Polaroid was so noisy.

"What was that?" the man says. "Gus, come here!" In seconds, two burly arms haul you out from your hiding place.

"Whaddaya got there, Hank?" asks a big, beefy blond you assume is Gus. "A photographer!" He rips up the photo you took. "Hey, kid, whaddya think you're doin'?"

Choices: You try to act tough with the man
(turn to page 83).
You tell them you don't want trouble
(turn to page 92).

You and your dad rush to Ms. Carson. You order Lapis to sit, and you drop to your knees beside the woman while your dad tells the crowd to back away. Genevieve hovers nearby, watching her mistress with head cocked to the side.

Angela's eyelids flutter open. "Wh-what happened?"

"You passed out," you say, "probably from the heat. But everything's going to be fine." You prop up her head a bit, using Lapis's grooming bag as a pillow. Dad reappears with a borrowed sun umbrella, which he sets up to shade her.

She tugs at your sleeve. "What about the show?" she says. "Isn't it about to start?"

"Yes, ma'am," says your dad, "but I don't think you should take part in it. We need to take you to the first aid tent, just to be safe."

Ms. Carson looks disappointed. Suddenly her eyes light up as she looks at you. "Why don't *you* show Genevieve for me?"

You gulp. "Me show Genevieve?"

Turn to page 80.

You turn back to the star map, but as you move your head, that dizzy feeling returns. Suddenly everything goes black. . . .

You wake up in bed, covered with white sheets. A hospital bed! What's going on?

Your mother is at your side in an instant. "You finally woke up! I was so worried! You've got quite a bump on your head."

"What happened?" you ask.

"I don't really know," she replies. "It seems you collided with that man on your bike in the dark, because his wife found you both knocked out cold on the sidewalk. What were you doing way over on Franklin Street, anyway?"

You're thinking that the crazy dream about a dog in a spaceship must have come from the bump on your head. Then you realize what your mother just said. "Franklin Street? What man?"

She points. There, in the next bed, is Big Ollie.

"You!" you splutter. "Here? But how . . . ?"

Big Ollie laughs. "Cat got your tongue? Or, should I say, *dog* got your tongue? Don't worry. We'll have plenty of time to talk." He winks again as a nurse comes and closes the curtain around his bed.

That sure didn't seem like the same Big Ollie you met last night. You guess that his experience changed him—for the better.

You've changed, too. At least you know you'll always look twice and wonder every time you see a dog.

THE END

"It'll be better than not entering her at all!" Ms. Carson insists. "I'll go to first aid *after* we show Genevieve."

Soon you're in the ring, wearing armband #38 and leading a white poodle!

"Take 'em around," says the judge.

The other poodles and handlers begin to walk. You hold the lead loosely, trying to walk at the right speed for Genevieve's short legs.

After everyone has circled the ring under the judge's watchful eye, he says "Stack your dogs." You crouch at Genevieve's side, extend her tail with one hand, and lift her chin with the other. The little poodle seems to know what to do: she stands there proudly, very still, even when the judge puts his fingers in her mouth to examine her teeth!

The judge backs up and looks over all the poodles again. Then he points his finger rapidly, three times. All the handlers and dogs start filing out of the ring, so you follow.

Suddenly Angela Carson runs up and throws her arms around you. "We won! We won!" she exclaims.

"We won?" you echo in a puzzled voice.

"Yes! The judge pointed at you first—for first place," she explains. She pushes you toward the first-place marker, where you're handed a ribbon and small trophy.

When you carry the prizes to Ms. Carson, she thanks you profusely for your help. "Now Genevieve qualifies to compete again later, but I'll be able to show her then. Let me pay you for substituting for me just now."

Choices: You accept the money gratefully (turn to page 141).
You accept the money gratefully (turn to page 141).

You tell Ms. Carson you won't take any pay (turn to page 114).
You tell Ms. Carson you won't take any pay (turn to page 114).

"We could pry the boards off a window," Diego suggests.

"No, wait!" You point up at an old metal fire escape. The bottom stair dangles above your reach, but you and Diego find a couple of boxes to stand on and soon are climbing the steps.

You rattle the door at the top of the steps. Locked. Diego tries a window a little lower down, and it opens.

You squeeze through the opening and find yourselves in a room containing only spider-webs and dust balls.

"We've got to find a way downstairs," you say quietly. You tiptoe through another room and into the hallway. There you see what seems to be the main staircase. "All right!"

"This place is spooky," Diego says. "Let's do our thing and then get out of here."

"Fine with me!" You start down the stairs at a run, cross the landing, and are halfway down the next flight when you realize Diego is way behind you.

You lean on the banister and look up. "Diego, what's taking you so—"

Crrrack! With a snapping, splintering sound, the old banister gives way beneath your weight. You're falling. . . .

Turn to page 88.

"Let go of me, you big creep!" you yell, trying vainly to pull free from Hank's grip. "I know what you guys are up to, and you'll never get away with it, 'cause I'm not the only one who knows! I have a partner, and—"

Almost without thinking, you turn toward the balcony where Jon is sitting. But you don't see him there.

"Yeah, sure, kid!" says Gus. "We know you're bluffing. You're coming with us now. We're going to have a little talk."

Choices: You act more cooperative (turn to page 92).
You kick Hank in the shins (turn to page 110).

"I don't think I can eat," you say. You're telling the truth; the sight of that strange food has you a bit nauseated.

Your mother looks at you knowingly. "Why don't you lie down in another room, then," she says. "Your father and I don't want to miss this meal." Mrs. Sherzad leads you to a bedroom in the house. You take your puppy in there and stretch out on the bed.

On the wall, you notice photos of men with turbans, carrying rifles. And not only men— some are boys who don't look any older than you. You also see a photo of the boy at the dinner table—Mr. Sherzad's son. If this is his room, he's certainly interested in his homeland.

The room is warm and dark, and your eyelids feel heavy. Your puppy has dozed off, so you decide it's safe to close your eyes. . . .

The next thing you know, Dad is shaking you by the shoulder. "Get up now. Time to go."

"What?" You rub your eyes and stumble after him to the car, waving good-bye to the Sherzads.

"You missed a good meal," Dad says as you all drive home. "And those slides were really something."

"I wish you could have been there for the boy, too," Mom adds. "He wouldn't say two words to the adults."

What can you say? Maybe you should have at least tried the food. If you didn't like it, you could have sneaked some to your dog!

THE END

The coach puts his arm on your shoulder and leads you away from the other players. "I wonder if you'd consider being team captain this year," he says.

You can hardly believe your ears. "Me?"

"Well," the coach continues, "I like the captain to be a good player—and you are. But, more importantly, the captain has to have the ability to lead and encourage the other players on the team. I think you've shown me that today."

"I'll—I'll try to be a good captain," you manage to say. When the coach leaves, you untie Midnight and start to run home. You can't wait to tell your parents the news.

You look at the black puppy trotting beside you. *It's amazing how much you can learn about life from a dog,* you think.

THE END

Feeling a little foolish, you crawl through the doorway after Sirius. To your amazement, once you're inside, there's room for you to stand up straight again. As a matter of fact, the inside of the doghouse isn't like the outside at all.

You're standing in a large, circular room painted a metallic green. The room seems empty except for a table in the center and a large screen on one wall. Sirius stands at the table—on his hind legs, as if that were his normal posture. He presses something under the tabletop, and a picture appears on the screen: a view of the dark yard outside the ship.

Suddenly a figure appears on the screen, lumbering across the yard toward you. You hear a surly voice.

"All right, you mangy mutt! I saw you sneakin' back here! You ain't getting no more food from us—I'll break your legs first. . . ."

"It's Big Ollie!" Sirius says. Quickly he presses something under the tabletop again, and a panel of buttons and levers appears. He pulls one. You feel a slight bump. On the screen you see first a blinding flash of light, and then nothing but a black, starry sky.

You have a funny feeling you know what happened, and Sirius confirms your fears. "Well, how would you like to go on a little trip, my friend?" he asks with a grin.

Turn to page 132.

You're falling through the air, but not for long. You land partway down the next flight of stairs and tumble all the way down to the second floor before you finally stop.

Diego hurries down after you. "Are you all right?" he asks.

You can hardly catch your breath. "I—think—I—bruised—my—ribs," you gasp. "And—ouch!—maybe—sprained my wrist."

"Now you know why I went so slowly," Diego explains. "You have to be careful in these old buildings."

Suddenly a door slams below you and a voice yells up the stairwell: "What's going on up there?"

You hear heavy footsteps ascending.

"I have a plan," Diego says. "Just let me do the talking, in Spanish. If anybody asks you anything, you answer in Spanish, too, okay?"

Choices: You agree to Diego's plan (turn to page 99).
You think you have a better idea (turn to page 118).

A couple of other kids yell at Trisha for missing the ball, but you keep quiet, remembering your mom's advice that praise is better than criticism. When the first half of the inning is over, you wait for Trisha and walk back to the bench with her.

"I blew it again," she says with a sigh.

"Wait a minute," you interrupt. "It wasn't a total loss. I know you're afraid of the ball—but you stood your ground, right? You didn't run."

"That's true," Trisha admits.

"Why don't you try for a little bit of progress at a time?" you suggest. "Next time a ball comes to you, see if you can stay put *and* keep your eyes open."

"Well, I don't know . . ." Trisha says.

You sigh. At least you tried.

Later in the game, a ball does go to Trisha. She keeps her eyes open, and her mitt actually stops the ball. It takes her forever to pick it up and throw it to the second baseman, but you overlook that.

"Way to go, Trish!" you call out. "You're coming along!"

Your team loses the game, but you don't feel too bad about it. You know at least one member of your squad is improving.

You're just about to untie Midnight and go home, when your coach approaches you.

Turn to page 85.

Jahan is about your age, tall, with olive skin, and hair and eyes nearly black.

"I had to get away from all the Christian jibber jabber," he says. "I am not Christian; I am Muslim. Anyway, I thought you might want to go outside and play with the dogs."

You pick up your puppy from his box and follow Jahan. "How come you're a Muslim? Your parents are Christians, right?"

Jahan sneers. "I'm old enough to disagree with what my parents believe, if I choose. Aren't you?"

You gulp. "I guess I never thought about it."

Outside you see a happier side of Jahan. He gets out two other Afghan puppies to play with yours. As you romp in the grass with the dogs, he laughs, his white teeth flashing.

Jahan picks up your pup and scratches him behind the ears. "Yes, I like this one," he says.

"Have you named him yet?"

"No," you admit. "I just haven't thought of anything."

"He is an Afghan hound, so use an Afghan name, not some silly American one. I hate America," Jahan says bitterly. "I hate the Soviet Union, too. As soon as I can, I'm getting out of here and going back to my country to fight the Russians. If I were there now, I'd be holding a rifle—I'm old enough."

You don't know what to say, so after a minute you mutter, "It's getting dark. We'd better go inside."

Choices: You think Mr. Sherzad should know about Jahan's feelings (turn to page 94).
You stay with Jahan (turn to page 105).

You try to make your voice sound young and scared—which isn't too hard at the moment. "Please don't hurt me," you squeak. "I just want my dog back." Even as you speak, you're being hauled toward the van.

Hank shoves you in the back and climbs in after you. Gus closes the doors and comes in through the driver's door. You look around the van's cargo area. The walls are lined with cages, and a couple have dogs in them. Fritz isn't in a cage yet, and he hops up onto your lap.

Meanwhile, Gus and Hank huddle together and consult in loud whispers. Finally Hank turns to you. "All right, kid. We know you didn't mean any harm. If you'll just forget what you saw a minute ago, you can have your little dachshund here back, and that'll be the end of it."

Quickly you nod in agreement.

Then Gus leans close and adds, "But if you say anything to anybody about this, just remember—we know where you live. And we can come back and make this little wiener dog of yours into sausage! So keep your mouth shut."

You shudder and nod again. Then, to your relief, Hank stands up and opens the back door, and you step outside with Fritz. You're still blinking in the sunlight when you hear the doors slam shut, and the van drives away.

Choices: You run into Jon's house (turn to page 104).

You try to follow the van (turn to page 112).

The next Saturday, Mr. Sherzad picks you up, and you head for the city. When you arrive in the Arab section, you feel as though you've traveled to the Middle East. Many of the shop signs and even street signs are in Arabic. Dark-skinned people crowd the sidewalk, some wearing long, flowing robes. Street vendors sell warm Middle Eastern "pocket bread" and other pastries.

As you walk, Mr. Sherzad points out a mosque. You had expected something with a fancy tower, as in Dr. Gruber's slides, but this is just a plain brick building.

Mr. Sherzad has a handful of Arabic pamphlets with him, and he gives you some. "Just hand these to people," he says.

Turn to page 126.

The slide show is over, and the adults are getting ready to leave. You pull Mr. Sherzad aside privately.

"Jahan says he is a Muslim," you whisper, "and that he hates America and—"

Mr. Sherzad motions you to stop. "I know all this already," he says. "We often go to the Arab section of the city to talk to people about Christ, but Jahan has also been hearing about Islam there. He does not know where he really belongs. Right now he is rebelling against my faith. That is hard, but I am also glad for it."

"You are?" you exclaim.

"Yes. I am glad he is thinking and asking questions," Mr. Sherzad explains. "It is easiest just to follow your parents' beliefs without examining them. But Christianity is not hereditary. Each person must believe in Christ for himself. All I can do is pray for Jahan. I hope you will pray, too."

You nod. Your parents are ready to leave, and soon you are all in the car, bumping along the road home. As you look out into the darkness, you realize that Jahan is right about one thing. You want to be a Christian, but not just because your parents are; you're old enough to think for yourself.

So you *will* think. And you hope you can talk to Jahan again.

THE END

You're still fuming about Trisha when its your turn to bat. Maybe your timing is off or something, but the pitches just fan you: three strikes and you're out.

"Way to go, slugger," you hear someone call out. Trisha.

You and the klutzy left fielder exchange a few more nasty comments that afternoon. You don't play very well, and your team loses. All in all, it's a rotten day.

As you untie Midnight and walk him home, you wonder how it all went wrong.

THE END

"Okay, Diego, I'll go home with you after school," you say. "If Hogan is really in that building, you'll get the reward."

When you return that afternoon, you bring some "tools" just in case you need them: paper and pencil and your Swiss Army knife.

The area looks run down. "We moved here from Mexico last year," Diego comments. "My parents don't earn much, but at least they have jobs. I'm going to summer school for my English."

"I think your English is good," you say honestly. "Say, I'm taking a Spanish class. Maybe we can help each other."

"Sure! Hey, here's the apartment building."

You look. The windows at the front are boarded up and the door is padlocked, with a No Trespassing sign posted on it. You also see a notice from the city, saying that the building is condemned.

"Maybe we can see some dogs through the windows around back," you suggest. You park your bikes at Diego's house, several doors down, and then return.

The back windows are boarded up, too, and the yard is surrounded by a high wooden fence. You manage to do a chin-up on the fence long enough to see inside—and you do see dogs.

You drop down and shake your arms. "I saw

four dogs," you tell Diego. "This place is definitely *not* abandoned."

"So, what do we do now?" Diego asks.

Choices: You try to get into the building (turn to page 82).

You go to Diego's house to plan (turn to page 103).

Just as you're passing the leash to your father, Lapis gives a mighty tug. The leather strap slips from your hand, and she's gone!

You whirl around in time to see her run off in the same direction as Genevieve. *Oh, no!* you think. *Now I've got two lost dogs instead of one!*

Turn to page 149.

Two men reach the landing where you sit. One is short and dark haired, the other a big, muscular blond.

"This is private property," says the short man. "You two have some explaining to do."

"Estábamos explorando, y mi amigo se cayó por la escalera," Diego begins, and then turns to you. *"Estás bien?"*

You didn't understand the first part, but you know the last two words mean, "Are you okay?"

"Sí," you respond, pointing to your arm. *"Pero mi brazo—"*

The dark-haired man turns to this muscle-bound partner. "It's just a couple of Mexican kids, Gus. They don't know anything. I'll kick 'em out—you lock all the windows upstairs."

"Okay, Hank." The big man steps over you to go on up the stairs.

Diego helps you down the stairs, but it's still a painful journey. At the front door, Hank grabs Diego by the collar and points to the sign. "No trespassing!" the man shouts. "Now, scram!"

You are only too glad to oblige. Hank comes outside also, and climbs into an orange van parked nearby.

Somehow the van seems familiar. Then you remember! "Diego, we have to make some phone calls!" you exclaim, hobbling more quickly now toward his house. "Ouch! Oh, my poor ribs . . ."

Turn to page 108.

Sirius presses a button, and two steaming plates appear, laden with something that looks like blue pudding. As you watch suspiciously, Sirius digs right in. "Boy, was I getting tired of that stuff you Earthlings call dog food!" he says.

You decide to shut your eyes and imagine that this stuff tastes like your favorite meal at home: roast beef, mashed potatoes and gravy, and carrots. You swallow. To your surprise, that's exactly what it tastes like! Sirius sees the question in your eyes and answers before you ask.

"This stuff is an illusion, too," he says. "It can taste like anything you want."

As the journey continues, you learn more about Sirius, his home, and his mission. As you suspected already, his civilization is highly advanced. "Our space travel is sophisticated now," he says, "but it wasn't always so. One exploratory expedition headed out to your solar system thousands of years ago, by your time, and was never heard from again. Only recently did we find out what had happened. The ship crashed somewhere in the Mediterranean Sea."

You wince. "I'm so sorry. What happened to the dogs?"

"A few survived, apparently," Sirius explains. "My guess is that they communicated with humans at first, enough so that the Dog Star became a part of Greek and Roman mythology, for example. But eventually those few specimens of my race became absorbed into your dog population—those poor dumb things on all fours."

"Poor dumb things!" you exclaim. "That's not a very nice way to talk about your relatives!"

"I don't mean to insult them," Sirius says with a sigh. "I just feel sorry for them. For centuries they've been kicked and beaten and thrown outside. Not very many humans have taken the time to think about the dogs' feelings. At least you do that. That's why I chose you to help me."

You're pondering his comment when suddenly some yellow lights on the instrument panel begin flashing.

Turn to page 107.

You bring up the topic at suppertime. "Mom and Dad, I'm having trouble training Midnight to go and wet outside. Do you have any ideas?"

"Well, let's see." Dad disappears into the family room, and your hear him rummaging among his books. Soon he's back with a frayed paperback he probably bought at a garage sale. "*Training Your Dog*," he says. "I thought it would come in handy sometime."

The book suggests watching the puppy closely, taking him outdoors frequently, and confining him in a small area indoors when he can't be watched.

You spread some newspapers on the kitchen floor and tie Midnight by his leash to the knob of a cupboard. Then you wander into the other room to watch TV.

"The Best of Johnny Carson" is on the screen—specifically, the show's annual singing dog contest. One by one, people are walking onstage, playing music, and letting their dogs howl along.

You know Midnight has quite a voice. If that singing dog contest awarded a prize, maybe Midnight could help pay for his own dog food. Or maybe there's another way he could earn his keep. . . .

Choices: You decide to train Midnight to sing (turn to page 106).
You think he's cute enough to pose for a dog food advertisement (turn to page 142).

You've gone only a few yards when you hear the sound of a motor behind you. You turn in time to see the back of an orange van as it pulls into the apartment drive.

Diego's eyes meet yours, and in silent agreement you turn and stroll casually back in that direction. As you pass the driveway, you hear muffled barking from the van. The vehicle seems to have writing on the side, but you can't read it from the sidewalk. You do memorize the license number. Then you cross the street to avoid suspicion and go to Diego's house again.

That orange van . . . something seems familiar about it. But why? You sit in Diego's kitchen, sipping lemonade, racking your brain. Then—

"Diego, I've gotta use the phone!" you exclaim.

Turn to page 108.

You burst through the door and run up the stairs. "Jon, did you see that?" you gasp.

"Saw it *and* taped it," Jon said. "Only the camera lens was sticking over the balcony—the rest of me was hiding. Boy, that was a close one!"

"Let's see the tape!" You watch it on his family's VCR. Jon's camera work couldn't have been better. He even focused in on the van's license number.

"That's the zoom lens," he explains proudly.

The police are pretty impressed, too, after you finally convince them to watch the tape. "Either that's a real dognapping," says one officer to another, "or these kids should be in Hollywood. Let's run down that address and do a search."

You go back to wait at Jon's house—but not for long. Pretty soon you have a chauffeured ride to your house, with your bike in the trunk.

Your mom has a pretty funny expression on her face when she sees you climbing out of a police car. But the newspaper headline next morning says it all: KIDS CATCH DOG THIEVES RED-HANDED. A photo of Jon next to the article is captioned, "Wheelchair Photographer Records Crime."

"This all turned out well, you know," Mom says later, "but you came pretty close to being kidnapped yourself!"

"Yeah, the police said what we did was too dangerous," you reply. "But don't you think I'm a little young to retire?"

THE END

You follow Jahan to his room, putting your puppy back in his box there, so he won't have any accidents on the floor. You notice now that the walls of Jahan's room reflect his interests. Besides photos of dogs, you see a map of Afghanistan and magazine photos of turbaned men with rifles.

"Those are the *mujahiddin,*" Jahan says proudly. "The freedom fighters. Someday I'll be one of them."

One other photograph on the wall catches your eye. It's a shot of Jahan sitting on a couch, taken from behind. He has turned to grin at the camera, and has his arm around someone with long, blond hair.

"Who's that?" you ask.

"Oh, that's my girl friend," Jahan says with a funny look in his eye. "I had the picture taken from behind us because she's so ugly."

You can't believe he really said that.

Choices: You quickly change the subject (turn to page 111).

You tell him he shouldn't talk that way (turn to page 144).

You stroll back out to the kitchen. "Midnight," you say, "would you like to learn to sing? Oowoo?"

"Ow, ow, owooo!" Midnight responds. It's a good start. Now, what song should you teach him?

"I have an idea," says your dad, strolling over to his record collection. "It's a folksy sort of thing on an old album I got at—"

"—a garage sale," you finish for him.

"It's called, 'Me and You and a Dog Named Boo,' by Lobo. Want to hear it?"

It's an easy, lilting kind of song—one that would go well with howling, you think. You make a tape of it, so you can play it on your cassette recorder.

The next day you begin "rehearsals." You set the recorder next to Midnight on the kitchen floor, and he sniffs it. When the music comes on, he jumps.

"Okay, Midnight, just relax and sing along," you say soothingly. "Like this: Ow, ow, owoooo." But the dog isn't making any sounds. You sing louder, trying to encourage him. Just then your friend Todd comes to the kitchen door.

"I never knew you had such a great voice," he says.

Choices: You decide to make Midnight famous some other way (turn to page 142). You say, "I don't care what anybody thinks—I'm teaching my dog to sing on TV" (turn to page 115).

"We're landing!" Sirius exclaims. "I'd better go put on my uniform." He rushes off, and reappears dressed in a headpiece and a sort of waistcloth that look strangely familiar.

"Let's go—everyone is waiting!" Sirius motions impatiently, and you follow him out the same door you crawled in a few hours ago. Or was it days? As you emerge into the sunlight, you see that the spaceship no longer looks like a doghouse, but is as round outside as inside. Its flattened, cylindrical shape reminds you of a tuna fish can.

But that shape doesn't surprise you nearly as much as the shapes of the buildings you see. Pyramids! Suddenly you realize why Sirius's costume looked so familiar.

He reads your thoughts once more. "Yes, I believe your ancient Egyptians learned some things from our people, too."

Then he turns and motions to two very large dogs. "The prisoner is inside. Take him to the dungeon." The dogs disappear into the ship and reappear dragging Big Ollie, who is blinking his eyes in terror and amazement.

Choices: You're glad the big bully can feel what it's like to have someone push him around for a change (turn to page 145). You feel sorry for Big Ollie, and ask Sirius what will happen to him now (turn to page 129).

The van looks like the one you saw the day you lost Hogan! It had said Animal Shelter on the side, but maybe the sign was a fake!

You dial the shelter on Diego's phone and explain your theory. The man on the other end remembers talking to you before, and he's disturbed by your report.

"We only have one van, and it's blue," he says. He agrees to call the police with your location and the van's license number.

You hang up and sigh. "Now we just wait."

"We could do my homework," Diego suggests with a grin.

"No way!" you reply. But then you agree to help, and an hour has flown by when you hear the doorbell. You run to answer it.

On the porch is a curly haired young man who smiles and says, "I'm Bill from the animal shelter, and I'd like to return—"

"Hogan!" you cry. Gently you take the puppy from Bill and cradle him in your arms.

Bill motions toward two squad cars stopped in front of the apartment building, lights flashing. "You were right on target, kids," he says. "Those guys were stealing dogs off the street. The purebreds they'd resell, but the others—" He shudders.

Just then a woman comes up the walk. *"Qué pasa?"* she asks Diego.

"Mamá!" he exclaims. They have a short conversation in Spanish, and then Diego turns to you. "Why don't you stay for supper? We're having burritos."

"Yum! I'll call home and ask." Right now you feel very blessed. You've not only found your puppy—you've made a new friend.

THE END

He only grunts and gets a firmer grip on you.

"I'm sorry you did that, kid," Gus says. "It would have been easier if you'd been more cooperative. As it is, you don't leave us any choice."

You wonder what he's talking about—until he goes to the front of the van and comes back with a hypodermic needle. You squirm, but it does no good: Hank has a grip like an iron clamp.

In seconds, everything goes black.

Turn to page 124.

"What do you think I should name the puppy?" you ask.

"You need to get to know him first," Jahan says, lifting the pup out of the box. "Would you like to bring him back here sometime? I could help you train him and teach him tricks."

You're surprised at the friendly offer. "I'd love to!"

Just then the puppy starts growling and turning round and round in a circle. Finally you realize what he's doing.

"The crazy dog is chasing his tail!" you exclaim, laughing.

"You could call him Dewana," Jahan suggests. "That means crazy. I guess it sounds kind of feminine in English, though."

Just then the lights go on again in the living room. Dr. Gruber must have finished showing his slides.

"Can you come back next week?" Jahan asks.

"I'll find out and call you," you promise. You put the puppy back in his box and start to leave. Then Jahan holds something out to you: a small book.

"Here's something you might like to look at before you come back," he says. "It's the Koran, the holy book of Islam."

Choices: You decline Jahan's offer, then rush out to his father (turn to page 94).
You accept the book (turn to page 36).

You tie up Fritz again. As soon as the van turns a corner, you start pedaling after it. You're able to keep track of it for a couple of blocks, but then it gets away from you.

You stop, discouraged. You're panting so loudly you don't even hear the sound of a vehicle pulling up behind you.

Then you feel one hairy hand clamped over your mouth, and another wrapped 'round your waist. "I thought we made a deal, kid," says a familiar voice. "I guess I was wrong about that."

Gus carries you to the van and shoves you in the back. "Should I tie him up, Hank?" he asks.

"No, I don't think we'll need to tie him," Hank replies. As Gus holds you firmly, Hank strides over with a hypodermic needle.

Everything goes black. . . .

Turn to page 124.

"I've got five dollars to put on my dog, Jet—the black one," you say proudly to the people behind you.

"Well, well," says the woman. "We'll see."

A gun sounds, the gates are opened, and they're off. At first Jet seems confused by all the other dogs and lingers by the starting line. You leap to your feet.

"Come on, Jet!" you scream, and off he goes.

But his speed doesn't make up for his late start, and Jet comes in fourth. Behind you, the owner of Big Red is collecting his money.

What a crummy way to spend five dollars.

You start down to the track to get Jet, when the woman behind you pats you on the shoulder. "I know how you feel," she says. "I lost ten bucks! Your dog did look good out there, though. Has he raced before?"

"No, he hasn't," you say.

"He looks familiar," she mutters. "Did his father race?"

"Why, yes!" you exclaim. "His father's name is Farouk."

The woman slaps you on the back. "Well, what do you know! Farouk has won many a race here. I hope I'll see you back. Maybe next time I'll lose my ten dollars to you!"

You just grin and wave at the woman. You may come back, and Jet may win. But you're not going to bet on it.

THE END

"Thanks, but I don't want to take any money from you, Ms. Carson," you say.

"Why not?" she asks. "If I'd hired a professional dog handler for Genevieve, I'd have had to pay him plenty!"

"Yes, but you didn't *plan* on spending money for that," you explain. "And Genevieve didn't win money just now, only honors. Anyway, I'm a Christian, and well, our pastor says we should act the way we think Jesus would. I'm just glad to be of help."

Ms. Carson raises her eyebrows when you mention Jesus, but doesn't comment. "Well, at least I can offer you a souvenir of the day," she says. She motions to a man nearby: the show photographer. He has you put Genevieve in her show stance again and hold up the ribbon; then he clicks the shutter.

Ms. Carson takes your name and address and promises to send you a copy of the photo. Then she waves good-bye and heads for the first aid tent.

Two weeks later, you get a large envelope in the mail. In it is an 8 x 10 black and white photo of you and Genevieve at the dog show and a note: "Thanks again for all your help. It's good to know there are some nice people in the world. Your friend, Angela Carson."

THE END

In spite of the teasing you get, you decide to keep up Midnight's "voice lessons." He's a bright dog, and seems to be catching on to the idea of howling along with the music.

A few days later, your dad runs into the kitchen, waving the newspaper at you. "You'll never believe it!" he says. "A TV station in town is having its own singing dog contest! It's being sponsored by Woofers Dog Food. Auditions are in two weeks."

"That's just what I'm looking for!" you say. "But tell me the truth, Dad. How do you think Midnight sounds? Is he good enough to enter?"

"He sounds good," your dad says. "But I think you ought to come up with something else to make your act impressive. You know, the song you've chosen isn't too hard, and you've had guitar lessons. Why don't you have Midnight howl along as *you* sing and play your guitar?"

You gulp.

Choices: You decide to give Dad's suggestion a try (turn to page 130).

You don't want to sing a solo in public, so you look for another way to boost your act (turn to page 151).

"I said, how did you know my name was Sirius?" the dog repeats.

"I didn't!" you stammer. "I didn't know Serious *was* a name!"

The dog looks relieved. "Why, yes. S-I-R-I-U-S. You know, the name of the Dog Star?"

"The Dog Star?"

"Haven't you studied astronomy? The Dog Star is the brightest star in the heavens. It's on the 'nose' of the constellation Canis Major," the dog says proudly. "So you see, my parents named me after—"

"Now just a minute!" you say. "Before you start giving me science lessons, I think you have some explaining to do!"

He sighs. "Yes, you're probably wondering why I can talk. Well, it's because I'm not a dog—at least, not an Earth dog. I come from another solar system. My planet revolves around the Dog Star, Sirius, just as yours goes around the sun."

"Then how did you get here?" you ask. "And why?"

"I came in a spaceship, of course," the dog replies. "My mission was to see what had happened to the others of my race who landed here centuries ago. Now I need to get back to my ship—and I need your help to get there."

Choices: You agree to take him where he wants to go (turn to page 51).

You want to ask a few questions first (turn to page 70).

"Dad, this van is blue!" you exclaim. "The one we saw earlier at the stoplight was orange. And the guy said he hadn't been in our neighborhood today, but he had—I saw him! And—"

"Now, hold on," your dad says. "The van could be from an animal shelter in another town, you know."

"Sure," you reply, "but then why would he lie about where he had been? I know it was an *orange* van I saw by our house. I think maybe they *stole* Hogan."

"Well, something does sound fishy," Dad admits.

You call the police when you get home and tell them about the van, but they say they can't help you. "We need more evidence of a crime here," says the voice. "There's no law against driving around in something orange."

You hang up frustrated. You're sure this orange van is connected to Hogan's disappearance, but what can you do? You go upstairs and glance through some of your favorite mystery and detective stories. There you find a couple of ideas.

Choices: You decide to keep track of the van's travels (turn to page 52).

You plan to bait a trap for the dognappers (turn to page 76).

"No, Diego, I have a better plan," you say. But there's no time to discuss it. Two men have arrived at the landing.

You and Diego both start jabbering at once, he in Spanish and you in English, but it's obvious the men are listening to you.

"Call the police!" you say. "This Mexican kid was trying to rob me!"

Diego's mouth drops open. The two men look at each other, obviously disturbed by your use of the word police.

Finally the short one says, "The police won't do anything to him, kid. How 'bout if Gus here roughs him up a little? That'll teach him a lesson."

You gulp. You can't bear to look in Diego's direction.

Choices: You say, "Yeah, beat him up" (turn to page 46).
You say, "No, I don't want him hurt" (turn to page 48).

"Well, how did the puppy do last night?" Mom asks at breakfast.

You grimace. "I'll give you a clue. I'm going to call him Midnight—and not just because he's black, either!"

Your father laughs. "I heard him whining. But give him a couple more days, and he'll get used to his bed."

He's right. After a few nights, the pup's crying stops. But then there are other crises to cope with. Midnight knocks over a plant, jumps on your mother's cream-colored living room chair, chews up your new loafers . . . and, of course, has accidents.

One day, you see a puddle on the kitchen floor. You've had it.

Choices: You drag the pup into the room and swat him, yelling, "You stupid dog!" (turn to page 38).

You ask your parents for help in training the puppy (turn to page 102).

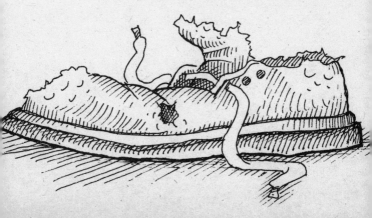

Jahan turns when he hears you yell. He finds you sprawled on the grass with your pup nosing in your pocket, gobbling treats.

His voice is low, but his eyes shoot fire. "I will not waste my time on someone who treats a dog that way," he says icily. "It's never necessary to yell like that."

"Well, I won't waste time with a dog that treats me that way!" you retort, getting up stiffly. "He's got to learn."

Jahan just turns back to his puppy as if you aren't even there. After a long silence, you decide you've had enough.

"We're going home," you say to your pup. "We'll just get our training someplace else."

As you head for the house, you realize something. If you and Jahan treated people the way he treats dogs, you'd both be better off.

THE END

"I'm sorry I can't give you the tour myself," Sirius continues. "I have meetings to attend and reports to give. But I've asked my friend Procyon to take you instead. I'll meet you later."

Sirius rushes over to a smaller tuna-can ship that seems to have been waiting for him. Its round, flat shape gives you an idea about your reward. As it flies off, you see that a reddish brown dog has appeared at your side.

"My name is Procyon," he says. "I'm your guide to the planet Veteri. Welcome."

"Thanks," you reply. "Say, I think I know what I want for my gift. I'd like to go see the rings of Saturn on my trip back to earth. Could I do that?"

"I'm sure you can," says your guide. "Saturn is a little out of your way—800 million miles or so—but that's not bad. Now let's see Veteri."

The two of you stroll toward another small, round ship. "By the way," says your new friend, "does my name sound familiar to you? Procyon is the name of a double star in the constellation you call Canis Minor. . . ."

Astronomy lessons again! You stifle a yawn and try to pay attention. Maybe if you improve your grade in science when you get home, your parents will let you buy another dog.

THE END

The woman whirls around, and then points to a man leaving the stands with something under his arm. "He's got my purse!" she shrieks. "Stop, thief!"

Suddenly you have an idea. You hold Jet's head in your hands and direct his gaze toward the purse snatcher. "Go fetch that purse, boy!" you say. "Go on. Run!"

You're not sure if Jet understood, but he takes off in the right direction, out of the stands and onto the field. The man had begun running when he heard the woman scream, and his flight draws Jet's attention. Jet gains on him quickly. The thief gives a terrified glance backward at your dog, drops the purse, and runs for his life.

You've run down from the stands, too, and now you call to the hound. "Here, Jet. Bring the purse here, boy."

The woman joins you as Jet comes panting up with the purse in his jaws and drops it at your feet.

"Thanks a lot!" she says. "You ought to sell that dog to the police department. Did you see the expression on that guy's face? He thought the dog was going to eat him!"

You both laugh. "I guess you got to race today after all, Jet," you say, scratching behind the dog's ears. "And you won, too. No question about it!"

THE END

The first thing you notice when you wake up is your aching head. The second thing is the smell—like a barn or worse. Where are you, anyway?

When your eyes adjust to the dim light, you realize that you're in a cage in a large room full of dogs, also in cages. That accounts for the smell.

The room is dark, except for light coming in through a low doorway leading outside. A few of the dogs—including Fritz—are running loose, going in and out of the doorway freely.

The yard outside must be fenced. You're surprised they let Fritz loose, though. It wouldn't take much digging for such a small dog to get under the fence and out.

You scrunch down on the bottom of your cage, trying to look out that doorway for clues to your location, but all you can see is grass.

Suddenly you hear a loud, long whistle. You've heard the sound before, but never so loud. Then you realize what it is—the signal for the end of a shift at the local plastics factory. It must be five o'clock.

At least you know where you are. You also know that many factory workers will be going home soon—maybe walking right by where you're imprisoned!

Choices: You yell for help (turn to page 136).
You try to send Fritz for aid (turn to page 150).

The crowd is so thick it's almost impossible to see where the toy poodle has gone. You crane your neck to look, while Lapis strains at her leash.

Suddenly the leather strap slips out from your sweaty fingers, and Lapis runs away from you. *Oh, no!* you think. *Now I've lost* two *dogs!*

Turn to page 149.

Soon a man who has taken a pamphlet comes back with a question. "The Koran says there is only one God. How is it that you Christians have three? Surely this is false."

Three gods? You guess he means the Trinity. You're glad Mr. Sherzad is answering, not you!

"We Christians also believe in one God," Mr. Sherzad explains. "But this God has three manifestations. A holy man from India, Sadhu Sundar Singh, once explained it like this: *'From the sun come both heat and light, and both are the sun, but their manifestation is in different forms. The light is not heat, and the heat is not light. So Jesus and the Holy Spirit, proceeding from the Father, bring light and warmth to the world. Yet they are not three, but one, just as the sun is one.'* "

Wow! That's quite an explanation. You think about it more as Mr. Sherzad and the man keep on talking.

Your day in the city is very interesting, but you're glad to get home again, where everyone speaks English!

Your pup seems glad to see you, too, and jumps up to lick you. He sure seems to have a happy disposition.

That gives you an idea. "I think I'll call you Sunny," you say. It seems to fit. Not only that—it will always remind you of your day as a "missionary."

THE END

You've found a more comfortable seat on the cushion, but that creates a new problem. Sirius's lecture is putting you to sleep. You're just nodding off for the third time when the sound of your name startles you awake.

"This human," Sirius is saying, motioning for you to stand, "took very fine care of me and risked personal safety in order to return me to my ship. I propose that the Canine Council grant my friend a choice of any gift, as a token of our appreciation."

You hear a chorus of low growls that apparently means the Council approves Sirius's idea. Soon your friend is at your side again.

"What would you like?" he asks. "A souvenir to take home from our planet? Perhaps a trip somewhere else in the galaxy?" Think about it while you tour Veteri."

Choices: You'd like to do more traveling (turn to page 121).

You'd like a souvenir to keep (turn to page 135).

"Me and you and a dog named Boo, travelin' and a-livin' off the land . . ."

You get through the song somehow and are relieved when it's over. Midnight did fine, but your chords didn't sound very good, and neither did your voice.

The other contestants are quite good. One has a poodle yipping along with "How Much Is That Doggie in the Window?" Another brings a bassett hound that croons along with—believe it or not—"You Ain't Nothing but a Hound Dog." You're not too surprised when the contest prize goes to someone else. You feel like sneaking out the back door and going into hiding for a week.

But before you can escape, the host calls all the contestants back on stage. "Let's give a hand to all our talented entrants!" he says. "They were all brave enough to come howl with their dogs for us—and we have a little something for them, too!"

The host's assistant then hands each contestant two T-shirts. "One for you and one for your dog," she explains. The one for you has the name of the TV station on it. Midnight's says "Woofers Dog Food."

Oh, well. You got to appear on TV and you won a free T-shirt. Maybe the contest was worth the effort after all.

THE END

"He'll get what he deserves," Sirius replies. "We believe in justice here. In prison he'll have a taste of what he used to do to his dogs—and to his wife and children, too. He'll have the rest of his life to regret his behavior."

"A life sentence?" you gasp. "But what about his family?"

Sirius scoffs. "They'll just think he left them. He's done it before. But cheer up, my friend: our justice is not all negative. We punish the bad, but we also reward the good. And you deserve a reward for all your help to me.

"First," Sirius continues, "I would like you to have a tour of our planet. As you tour, think about what you would like. Some sort of souvenir from here? Or perhaps a trip somewhere else in the galaxy? I'm sure the Canine Council will grant you anything."

Choices: You start thinking about what kind of gift you'd like (turn to page 121).
You're too shaken by Big Ollie's fate to think about a reward (turn to page 140).

You only have two weeks to prepare so you get to work right away. It's not easy to get your fingers going because you're out of practice, but Midnight soon catches on to singing with your guitar instead of a tape.

In no time, the big day arrives. You wear bib overalls and a floppy hat to fit the hobo theme of the song, and Midnight has a bandana around his neck. Your dad drives you to the tryouts.

Soon your name is called, and you and Midnight walk onstage.

"Go ahead," says a voice from behind the blinding spotlights.

You clear your throat and start strumming. "Me and you and a dog named Boo, travelin' and a-livin' off the land . . ." On cue, Midnight joins in. As you leave the stage, a show representative invites you to come back for the real, televised contest the next day!

The atmosphere is more tense this time, and so are you. You see the TV cameras, the host, and the members of the show's band.

Suddenly, it's your turn. You walk from the semidark waiting area to the blinding lights of the stage. You sit down, introduce yourself, and fiddle one last time with your guitar.

Twang! A guitar string snaps in two.

Choices: You try to play with only five strings
(turn to page 128).
You ask the guitar player in the band if you can borrow his instrument **(turn to page 74).**

Your dad drops to his knees at Angela Carson's side while you lunge toward Genevieve, trying to grab her leash. But your sudden move frightens the toy poodle, and she bolts away!

Choices: You hand Lapis's leash to your dad and run after Genevieve (turn to page 98).

You take Lapis with you as you go after the poodle (turn to page 125).

"A trip!" you exclaim. "To where?"

"To my home planet, the planet Veteri," Sirius replies. "You can spend a couple days there and then go home."

"A couple of days!" you gasp. "What about my parents? They'll think I've been kidnapped or something."

Sirius laughs. "They won't even know you were gone. Space travel has peculiar effects on time. You could be gone a couple of days, and only a few minutes will have passed on Earth."

"Okay, you win." You decide to relax and enjoy the trip. So many things are different than they seem: a doghouse that's really a spaceship, days that really are minutes.

Dinner is a surprise, too. Sirius brings you a steaming plate of something that looks like blue pudding, but tastes like your favorite meal: roast beef, mashed potatoes and gravy, and carrots.

After dinner Sirius goes to another room and reappears wearing a familiar-looking headdress and a sort of skirt.

The landing on Veteri is so smooth you barely feel it. With Sirius you walk out the ship's hatch into the sunlight. A crowd of other dogs, all dressed like Sirius, surrounds the ship. You look beyond the crowd to the city. The buildings are shaped like pyramids! Now you know why Sirius's costume looked familiar.

Your friend reads your thoughts. "Yes," he says with a smile. "I guess the Egyptians picked up a few ideas from us. Come with me now. I have to appear before the Canine Council to report on my mission. Then I can give you your tour."

The two of you step into the Veterian version of a limousine: a small flying ship shaped something like a can of tuna. It speeds along just a few feet above the ground and soon gets you to your destination: a gigantic statue of a dog that reminds you of the Sphinx. You and Sirius pass through a doorway between the statue's paws and come into a large chamber inside. The auditorium is filled with low cushions, not chairs. Though Sirius and his kind seem to stand like humans do, you notice that they sit and lie like Earth dogs.

Sirius goes to the front of the chamber and soon is called on to speak. You find a cushion in the back of the room and try to listen, but his report drags on and on.

Choices: You change your position and try to pay attention (turn to page 127).
You decide to slip out the door and do a little touring on your own (turn to page 153).

You've just realized that you've seen two sides of Jahan. When he talks about his country or about religion, he's angry and rebellious. But with dogs, he's patient and loving. Suddenly, this ties in with something you read about Islam.

"Jahan, did your ever think that God's care for people is like our training of puppies?" you ask.

Jahan looks at you. "You're *dewana*," he says.

"No, really!" you say. "Your god, Allah, has such high standards for you to meet, so many rules. If you don't meet them, he doesn't help you or forgive you. The Christian God has high standards, too, but he's patient when we fail. He forgives us. He wants to help us to do better. He loves us—just like you love your dogs."

You can see Jahan is listening. Finally he says, "I had never thought of things that way. But I have thought of something else: a name for your dog."

"What's that?" you ask.

"*Dost.* That means friend." The way Jahan says it, you know he means that *you* are his friend, too.

"*Dost.* It's different, but I like it, you say." You look down at your pup. "Okay, time to get back to work. Sit, Dost. Sit! Good boy!"

THE END

"I'd like something solid to remember all this by," you say.

Sirius assigns you a tour guide, who whizzes you past the city's pyramids to the flat, green countryside. You see rivers, lakes, and crops, but no livestock or factories. Your guide explains that his race are vegetarians. Much of their industry is conducted underground. "Easier to heat and cool there," he says.

When your tour is over, you meet Sirius at his home, a domed structure with most of its rooms below ground. There you see what you'd like to take home: a small picture of a Veterian dog in front of a pyramid. Sirius wraps it for your return trip.

In no time at all you're back on Earth, standing by your bicycle and looking at the night sky. You pedal home, clutching your gift from Sirius, and go straight to bed.

When Mom comes to wake you in the morning, she notices the picture. "Where did you get this?" she asks.

"From a friend," you explain. "I did him a favor, and he wanted to thank me."

At breakfast, you explain that your dog is gone. "I found the home he came from. He wanted to go back."

"That's too bad," Mom says. "Do you want to go over to the animal shelter and find another?"

You shake your head. "There will never be another dog like him," you say sadly. And it's true—there never will.

THE END

"Somebody help me! I've been kidnapped!"

The dogs are startled by your voice, and a few start barking. The sound echoes in the room. Probably no one can hear you above their howls. At least Gus and Hank don't seem to be home.

You try yelling gain, but the same thing happens. Shouting is tiring, and you can't shout louder than the dogs, anyway. Then it hits you: if the dogs bark louder than you yell, why not bark?

"Grrruff!" you say. "Bowwow!" Soon all the dogs in the room are yipping and howling. The sound is deafening. When they quiet down, you growl or meow to start them off again.

Your throat is feeling very raw when suddenly you hear a door opening and footsteps. "Look at all these dogs! No wonder the neighbors complained—hey, look here, Bruce!" A pair of legs

in blue trousers appears by your cage, and then a woman's head topped with a police hat. "What's your name, honey?" she asks.

You try to reply, but nothing comes out. Your voice is gone. Then you remember the paper and pencil in your jeans pocket. You pull them out and start writing.

Soon you're home in bed, on doctor's orders, to recover from laryngitis and from the shot Gus gave you. The doctor says you're lucky; some animal tranquilizers are fatal to humans.

Hogan keeps you company. The little beagle seems none the worse for his dognapping experience. As a matter of fact, he *slept* through the barking you and the other dogs did.

"Typical puppy," says your mom. "Now, take your medicine."

THE END

A gun sounds, the gates are opened—and they're off. At first Jet seems confused by all the other dogs and lingers by the starting line. You leap to your feet.

"Come on, Jet!" you scream, and off he goes.

The track is a blur of bounding dogs, in all colors of fur and silk. You can see that Jet is one of the faster ones, but his speed doesn't make up for his late start. He comes in fourth.

You start down to the track to get him. "Good boy!" you say. Next to you a man is removing the muzzle from a golden Afghan in a green racing silk.

"First race?" the man asks.

You nod glumly.

"Don't feel bad," he continues. "He ran well. He just needs more practice with other dogs."

"Jet comes from a family of racers," you say proudly. "His father was Farouk."

"Really? Well, what do you know!" the man exclaims. "I've seen old Farouk win a few races here. Would you like to bring your dog back for some practice runs with other dogs?"

"I'd love to!" you exclaim. You scribble your name and phone number on a piece of paper, and the man promises to call.

Jet didn't win, but somehow you feel like celebrating. At a concession stand you buy two ice-cream cones.

"Here you go, Son of Farouk," you say to Jet. "One for me, and one for you!"

THE END

You swallow hard to keep from yelling Hogan's name. "A dog business. That's nice," you manage to say. "Maybe Diego and I got carried away imagining some big criminal stuff going on here. We're sorry."

"I'm glad you learned your lesson," says Hank. "Just go on home now. It says No Trespassing on the door, and we mean it."

You and Diego are only too glad to get out. As soon as you're clear of the apartment, you say: "Let's go to your house right away and make some phone calls!"

"Just a minute." Diego turns to you with a very sober expression. "I'm not quite ready to let you in my house yet."

"Why not? Oh." You remember now. "I really put you on the spot there, I know. I just thought maybe we could get the police there that way. I thought the two guys might believe you were a thief because you're—"

"Because I'm Mexican?" Diego asks. "If people believe that, it's because of prejudice. The whole thing didn't seem funny to me at all. You almost had me beat up!"

You're silent a minute. Then you say, "I'm sorry, Diego. I guess I have a lot to learn."

To your surprise, Diego flashes you a shy smile. "Okay," he says. "Let's go home now."

As you walk, you pass an orange van parked in the apartment driveway. For some reason, it looks familiar to you.

Turn to page 108.

Sirius notices your agitation. "What's the matter?" he asks. "Isn't your reward big enough?"

"You know, Sirius," you say, "justice isn't always the very best thing. My planet is full of jails and prisons, but they don't *help* people— they just punish them. Sometimes the best thing is mercy: giving people a chance to change inside, to do better."

Sirius looks at you curiously, but you go on. "God doesn't just give people what they deserve, he gives them another chance. That's what I want to do. Sirius, as a gift to me, I want you to let Big Ollie go."

The dogs around you gasp, but Sirius nods. "I said I would grant what you want, so I will."

Soon you and Big Ollie are taken on a brief tour of the planet. Then it's back to the ship for the journey to Earth.

Ollie doesn't speak to you at all during the tour or the trip home, and you begin to wonder if you should have freed him.

The ship leaves you in his yard. It's still dark; little Earth time has passed since you left.

Finally Big Ollie breaks the silence. "Kid," he says, "I've learned something, and I have you to thank. Tomorrow morning, I'm goin' to the animal shelter to get me a new dog. And this time, I'm gonna treat it right."

You grin at him. "You know, I've been wanting to get a dog myself. Maybe we can go to the shelter together."

THE END

"It's the least I can do," she says with a smile. "You acted just as a professional handler would, and they get paid. You did a good job, too. You're a real natural with dogs."

She presses some bills into your hand and walks away to find the first aid tent.

You open your palm and look at the money. Two ten-dollar bills! It's great—every little bit helps toward the expense of feeding and grooming Lapis.

But you're even more excited by Ms. Carson's remarks. A natural with dogs? Maybe a job as a professional dog handler could be in your future.

THE END

Maybe you're prejudiced, but you think Midnight is an awfully cute puppy. He's certainly as cute as the dogs you see pictured on the bags of dog food at the grocery store. Maybe you and Midnight can earn a little money through a modeling career.

You always feed Midnight Woofers Dog Food, and you think the company might like to photograph a puppy that really eats their product. You search the outside of the dog food bag and finally find the company address. You write and ask about getting Midnight into their ads.

In a couple of weeks, you receive the following letter:

Dear Customer,

Thank you for your interest in the Woofers Dog Food Company. You asked about having your dog appear in advertisements for our product. To learn about this, you will have to write to our advertising department. Perhaps you could send a photo along with your letter. Since you do not live in our city, the advertising department may not be able to use you, but you can always try.

> *Sincerely,*
> *Elaine Franz*
> *Customer Service Department*

You do as Ms. Franz suggests and send in two photos: one of Midnight, and one of you and Midnight together. You enclose them with a letter explaining how happy and healthy Midnight is because he eats his Woofers every day.

You can imagine the finished ad already. Your photograph and letter are splattered across millions of magazines. You're rich! You're famous! When you get another letter back from the Woofers Dog Food Company, you tear it open eagerly.

Dear Customer:

Thank you for your interest in advertising for Woofers Dog Food. We're always glad to hear from satisfied customers. We are sorry to say that we cannot use your photographs, however. We already have contracts with professional photographers and agencies to do our work. We do hope you will continue your word-of-mouth advertising of Woofers. We've enclosed a coupon to help you get started.

You sigh and glance at the coupon. The advertising business is a lot more complicated than you had realized. Oh, well—at least you learned something. And you get a free bag of dog food out of the deal, too: Woofers, of course.

THE END

"I can't believe you call your girl friend ugly!" you exclaim. "That's really rude!"

Jahan isn't at all upset by your reaction. In fact, he's fallen back onto his bed because he's laughing so hard. Finally he catches his breath and says, "I was only kidding. That's not my girl friend. That's a dog!"

"What?" You look at the photograph again. Yes, Jahan could be right. You don't see any face or even shoulders in the picture—just the back of a head covered with long, golden hair. And Afghan hounds have long hair.

"Great idea, isn't it?" Jahan says.

"Yeah! Do you think I could get a photo like that of me with my dog?" you ask.

"Sure, when he's older. I'll help you."

You see the lights go back on in the living room. The slide show must be over, so you'll be going home soon. But you and Jahan make plans to get together again, and Jahan offers to help you train your puppy. It's funny: at first you didn't like Jahan, but now you see that he has many sides to him.

On the way home, you think about Jahan's trick photo. When you get one like it, you're going to put it on the inside of your locker at school. You start chuckling aloud at the thought.

"What's so funny, dear?" your mom asks from the front seat.

"It's hard to explain, Mom," you say. "You'll find out soon enough!"

THE END

"Well, it looks like he's getting what he deserves," you say to Sirius, as the guard dogs lead Big Ollie away.

"Precisely," says your friend. "On our planet, we believe in justice. He is punished for his evil deeds toward me, and you will be rewarded for your good deeds."

A reward? You don't know what to say.

"First," Sirius continues, "I would like you to have a tour of our planet. As you tour, think about what you would like. Some sort of souvenir from here? Or perhaps a trip somewhere else in the galaxy? I'm sure the Canine Council will grant you anything."

Turn to page 121.

Jahan turns and finds you sprawled out on the grass with the pup nosing in your pocket for treats.

"I wish I had a camera right now," he says with a grin.

"Very funny," you say. "I think I'm a failure as a dog trainer. This pup hasn't learned a thing."

Jahan shakes his head. "You're doing fine. You just need to keep at it. Training a dog requires a lot of patience and love. And you need to keep praising the dog, too."

As Jahan goes back over to his puppy, something dawns on you. You feel as if a light bulb just clicked on inside your head.

Turn to page 134.

Diego blushes and says, "I thought I would meow. That will make the dogs bark, and maybe somebody will come to see why."

You're not sure this will work, but you know Diego deserves your cooperation. He meows, and you decide to bark. Sure enough, the dogs all join in. They make a terrible racket.

Then, above the noise of barking, you hear a woman's voice.

"Diego! Donde estás!?"

"That's my mother!" Diego cries. "When I count to three, yell *'Aquí, Mamá, aquí!'* "

You do as he says. Soon her voice comes closer, and Diego tells her to get the police.

An hour later you're back home, explaining the whole thing to your parents. "Diego's mom has a bit of detective in her, too," you conclude. "She saw his bike, but couldn't find him. He'd been curious about the apartment before, so when she heard the dogs barking there, she thought he might have something to do with it."

"Now, I know the police and the animal shelter appreciated your help," Dad says in a lecturing sort of tone. "But you put yourself in some pretty dangerous situations."

"Yeah, I did some stupid things," you admit, petting your puppy's head. "But I've learned my lesson. Hogan and I will do safer things now, like hunting rabbits or something."

"Poor bunny rabbits!" says Jenny, as you give your folks a wink.

THE END

Everyone turns and stares at you.

"You know what, Hank?" Gus says. "I think these two were playing detective all right—and we just showed them what they were looking for. Now what'll we do with them?"

"I'll have to think about it," Hank says. "But right now we have more work to do. Let's lock 'em up."

Before long, you and Diego are side by side, each in your own dog cage. Hank and Gus go out again, leaving you alone.

"Some friend you are!" Diego says. "First you call me a thief and almost get me beat up. Then you open your mouth and get us locked into cages."

"I know. I was stupid," you admit, "but let's not talk about that now. They locked us in these cages with padlocks. How are we going to get out of here?"

"Well, let me do the planning this time," Diego says. "Your ideas aren't working so well."

"All right, all right," you agree. Then you're both silent. For a while, neither of you can think of *anything* to do.

Then, at the same time, you both shout, "I've got an idea!"

Choices: You say, "My idea really *is* good this time" (turn to page 152).

You say, "Okay, Diego, we'll try your idea" (turn to page 147).

At least Lapis is bigger and easier to see than Genevieve. You race after her, dodging bodies as the pup bounds across the crowded field.

Suddenly you break out of the mob into an open area. Lapis is ahead of you, and beyond her is Genevieve, running for the parking lot!

But Lapis's long legs close the gap quickly. She runs between Genevieve and the parking lot, and you hear her barking and snapping.

You run to pull the two dogs apart. As soon as you grab Genevieve's leash, Lapis quits growling and wags her tail.

"Why, you rascal!" you exclaim, rubbing Lapis's shaggy head. "You started a fight on purpose, so I could catch up to you two!"

Soon you're back at the ring. Angela Carson is sitting under a sun umbrella next to your father, but when she sees Genevieve she runs and scoops the poodle into her arms.

"You won't win any shows today," she says, examining the dust on Genevieve's white coat, "but I'm sure glad to see you!"

When you explain what Lapis did, she says, "Afghans have good eyes and fast legs—but your Lapis is pretty smart, to boot!"

You just grin and pat your dog again.

"Neither of us will be showing our dogs today," Ms. Carson continues, "so why don't we have lunch and then watch some other breeds compete? I'll treat you: it's the least I can do."

"Sounds good to me!" you say.

THE END

"Here, Fritz!" you say. "Here, boy!" The little dog trots over to you, and you give him part of a candy bar you have. Then you find pencil and paper in another pocket, and write a note. "Help! Imprisoned in building near factory."

You sign the paper, then wrap it securely around Fritz's collar. "Fritz," you say, "go dig a hole. Go home to Jon!"

Fritz trots outdoors. You wait a long while, and then call to him—but he doesn't come.

You finish off the candy bar and lie down in the cage. The minutes seem to crawl by. Outside, the daylight fades.

Suddenly you hear some sounds, and then Hank and Gus talking. Your heart sinks. But then there are shouts and the sounds of a scuffle.

Finally someone opens the door to the room where you are. "We're the police. We're here to help you," a voice calls.

In a couple hours you're home in bed, recovering from the tranquilizer Hank gave you. The doctor said you were lucky—some animal tranquilizers can be fatal to humans.

Jon tells you how Fritz dug his way out and was picked up by the *real* animal shelter. His tags led them to Jon, who had already called the police. Your note helped them find you.

"His picture will be in tomorrow's paper," Jon says proudly. "Fritz the wonder dog!" You smile and scratch Hogan. Your pup is back safely and that's wonderful enough for you.

THE END

"Dad, I can't play my guitar onstage like that! I quit lessons six months ago. But I have another idea. That dog food name, Woofers, makes me think of woofers and tweeters—you know, those things in audio speakers?"

Your dad nods, and then you explain your plan.

Two weeks later, you and your dad and Midnight are at the TV studio, waiting your turn to audition.

"You realize that you're not being filmed," a station employee explains. "These tryouts are held to pick the best contestants for the televised contest."

"Next!" another voice calls out.

It's your turn.

Turn to page 28.

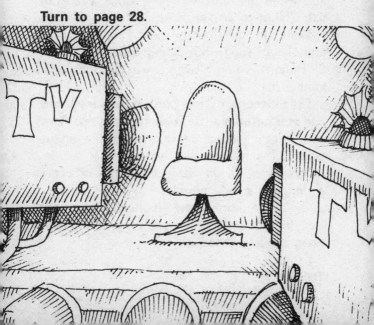

Diego agrees to listen.

"This is foolproof," you say. "We can undo the door hinges! I've got a Swiss Army knife in my back pocket. If you could reach it. . . ."

After some squirming, Diego works the knife out of your pocket and gives it to you.

You flip out the screwdriver portion of the knife and start unfastening hinges. In no time you're out, and you start on Diego's cage. Then the two of you stumble out of the building and into the sunlight.

From Diego's house you call the police. They come in an unmarked car and, after talking to you, decide to sit and wait for Gus and Hank to return. They tell you to go home.

You're too nervous and excited to eat supper, and when the doorbell finally rings, you're up like a shot to answer it.

There, on your doorstep, stand a police officer and Diego. Diego is holding something. . . .

"Hogan!" you cry. Eagerly you take the pup in your arms.

The officer introduces himself to your parents, and you introduce your new friend Diego. Then your mom serves ice cream while everyone takes turns telling what happened.

Too soon, Diego has to go; the officer is giving him a ride home.

"I'll see you tomorrow—*manana*," you promise. "For one thing, I want to give you your reward. You earned it!"

THE END

Quietly, you get up and go out. To the left you see pyramids and to the right you see smaller domed structures—probably the residential section. You head that way.

As you enter the first cluster of domes, you see some puppies playing. They're so cute you want to run up and hold one, but when you approach, the pups look at you in fear and run away. Soon you hear the hum of a small ship coming. Two large dogs hop out, stride over, and grab you roughly.

"Stray extraterrestrial, all right," says one.

"No identification, either," says the other. "Guess we'll just have to take him in and see if anyone claims him."

No amount of protesting can change their minds. Soon you're in a cage next to a short green creature with three eyes. At least the guard on duty believes your story about knowing Sirius, and calls him. When Sirius arrives, the guards let you go.

"I'm sorry," you say. "I shouldn't have gone off alone."

"True," he agrees, "but I should have given you this." He hands you a thin strip of leather with several engraved pieces of metal attached to it. "If you get lost again during your stay on Veteri, you won't have the same problem."

"What is it?" you ask.

"Your collar and tags, of course," Sirius replies, laughing.

THE END